Marina Tsvetaeva

SEAGULL
BOOKS
·
CELEBRATING
40 YEARS

THE FRENCH LIST

Vénus Khoury-Ghata

MARINA TSVETAEVA

To Die in Yelabuga

Translated by Teresa Lavender Fagan

LONDON NEW YORK CALCUTTA

**PAP
TAGORE**

www.bibliofrance.in

The work is published with the support of the
Publication Assistance Programmes of the Institut français

Seagull Books, 2022

Originally published as *Marina Tsvétaïéva, mourir à Elabouga*
© Mercure de France, 2019

First published in English by Seagull Books, 2022
English translation © Teresa Lavender Fagan, 2022

ISBN   978 1 80309 063 4

British Library Cataloguing-in-Publication Data
A catalogue record for this book is available from the British Library

Typeset and designed by Seagull Books, Calcutta, India
Printed and bound by Hyam Enterprises, Calcutta, India

To Tzvetan Todorov

What if your excesses were only a frantic quest
For happiness never to be found?

Looking out the tiny garret window you see the hill, the cypress, the field you explored every nightfall digging for potatoes the farmers might have left behind. You ate the peelings and kept the inside for Mur, who was always hungry.

So skinny, your son, you could see his bones through his skin.

A hill turning blue, then disappearing with the light, a cypress planted along a winding road to nowhere, a field transformed by the melting snow into an ocean of mud.

The window, your only connection to the world since you are no longer able to put words to your pain, since you are no longer loved, and you no longer prepare food.

The field replaces your blank page, its furrows written lines, the cypress your pencil.

The window and the garret belonged to the former owner of the property who died during deportation, the chair belongs to the Tatars who don't speak your language. You brought the rope.

Attached to the beam above, the slipknot is ready.

'It's a good thing she hung herself,' Mur would say; he wouldn't attend your burial in the Yelabuga cemetery, a tossing of stones from the furrows you searched with your hands looking for frozen potatoes.

'Thief', a 'dirty thief', the owner of the field shouted at you yesterday. The potato hidden behind your back, you told him you were sorry, but didn't return the object of the infraction.

Mur shrugged when you told him what had happened.

Mur acted like he hadn't heard when you told him you could no longer endure your life and were going to hang yourself.

You wouldn't have hanged yourself if your son were not so hungry, if you had a table where you could write and if you had news of your husband and daughter Alya, both accused of spying for the enemy. Arrested more than a year ago. Perhaps executed.

You wouldn't have hanged yourself if you hadn't been so cold, if you had gotten off at Chistopol instead of continuing on to Yelabuga in the truck that transported writers fleeing the German army.

Maybe you wouldn't have hanged yourself if Boris Pasternak hadn't abruptly ended a five-year correspondence during a five-minute encounter in the Moscow subway. If Rilke had answered your impassioned letters, if you hadn't exhausted the patience of the young critic Bakhrakh, if your Berlin publisher Abraham Vichniak hadn't returned your love letters without a word of explanation.

You wouldn't have hanged yourself if you were less miserable, if you could still write, and if the handsome Konstantin Rodzevich, your husband's best friend, hadn't ended your affair.

Long, the list of your passions, your infatuations, whether experienced or expressed in writing.

You wrote and loved like a prisoner who bangs on the wall separating himself from another prisoner. To sense you belonged to this world in which in fact you were alone. Alone and destitute, with a wealth of words you dispensed in all directions.

A beam, a rope, a chair, and your heart turned to stone through so many trials. You look from the slipknot above your head to the black mud undulating up to the cypress and the hill suddenly blanketed in darkness.

What are you waiting for?

It would take only someone calling out, a hand knocking at your door, for you to get down off the chair, throw the rope back over the beam, postpone your hanging, that word often repeated, as you have always planned to choose the date of your death. To stay ahead of it.

Indecision saps all your energy. You are unable to get down off that accursed chair, as if there are nails attaching your feet to it, feet that have suddenly become motionless, whereas your hands continue to move, making a gesture you always made when confronting any difficulty.

With the back of the right hand, you strike the air above your shoulder.

'What will come, will come,' says your hand.

An old hand, ruined from digging in the ground, wringing rags, sweeping tenacious dust that returned as soon as your back was turned. When you walked in front of mirrors, you closed your eyes so you wouldn't see the wrinkles as deep as valleys, the protruding veins, the skin as cracked as the bark of an old tree.

The smooth, new hand of a child rises up under your eyelids. It clutched your skirt at the door of the orphanage where you placed your daughters so they could fill their bellies, at least that's what they had told you, it grasped your skirt when you were rushing to return home with her sister who was sick, possibly dying.

The feverish patient wrapped in a horribly filthy blanket, you left the place without looking back at the little girl who was screaming her sister's name, not yours, a name difficult for her delayed brain to produce.

Irina the little-loved one paced around you like a puppy begging to be caressed. Irina the plucked bird, her head shaved to ward off the lice.

The orphanage gate closed behind you, she struck her head on the ground in the rhythm of a metronome.

There was no time for pity. You had to find the road back to Moscow, find it in the thick fog, in the night which had fallen sooner than usual. In the snow which had become stony. You had above all to escape the little hands that clutched your skirt.

Saving Alya from death was your priority, your reason for living.

A gifted child, at the age of eight Alya wrote in her journal whereas Irina at four couldn't talk and still wet herself.

Fed by whatever charitable souls left at your door, warmed with wood gathered in the woods, after a month Alya was able to stand up. With her malaria overcome, you remembered the 'other' and you returned to the orphanage.

'Irina is dead,' a boy told you as soon as you arrived. Dead from starvation and neglect like the other children. Two bowls of soup of hot water for the two daily meals, a cabbage leaf in the first, lentils in the second, counted out to make the pleasure last.

Dead and buried in her dirty pink dress that she had worn for the last two months, but without her blond hair; her head shaved like that of a prisoner.

It has been 20 years since her death, you try not to think of it, bring it up only if necessary, rarely utter her name.

'Left on 27 November 1919 for the orphanage in Kuznetsovo, a village outside Moscow where children are supposed to be well fed,' you write in your journal,

> Some clothes, two books, and a notebook for Alya dressed for the cold. Irina wears the same dress.

Kneeling in front of your eldest, you told her to eat as much as possible. And especially not to forget her mama.

'This is all just a game,' you told her. 'You'll pretend to be the little orphan. Your head will be shaved, you'll wear a long, pink, dirty dress down to your feet and a number around your neck when you should be living in a palace and not in an orphanage. A game, do you realize how extraordinary it is? It will be a great adventure, the greatest of your childhood. You understand, Alya, and tell yourself that I love only you.'

Not a word to Irina who wouldn't have understood anyway, her brain of a bird understood the opposites of things, otherwise she would have been frightened by the snowstorm that almost turned over the sleigh, wouldn't have clapped at the sight of the grey and gloomy façade of the orphanage. A month without asking about her. Your thoughts, your embraces reserved for Alya. Irina could wait.

You can see her blond hair, her thin neck, her filthy dress, stiff as cardboard.

Being hungry didn't stop her from singing her little song. Singing when hunger kept her from sleeping, her friends told you.

You should have brought her back home with her sister, in spite of the close quarters and the dishes piled up in the sink, made a little place for her in your 15 square meters, given her a pinch of the love you had for Alya.

Not enough room in your heart for both girls. You rationed Irina's share to feed Alya, clothed Irina with Alya's castoffs. Never hugged her.

How can you survive such images, forget Mur's insults yesterday, your summons from the NKVD to appear tomorrow, forget that your husband and daughter 'are no longer on the list of prisoners', so, executed, forget that your poetry can't be published because it doesn't conform to the Communist aesthetic, and that you have no access to work except perhaps as dish-washer in the writers' canteen.

You don't know if you should keep living or die.

'Thief', the farmer's shout cuts through the air of Yelabuga, his face floats above a furrow. Visible through the window, he repeats the word thief a second time as if once wasn't enough.

Your foot pushes the chair under your feet, you are at the mercy of the rope. The world becomes smaller as it tightens around your neck. The farmer, the hill, the field disappear in a whirl. The last to go: the cypress carved like a pencil, symbol of your short life.

Hunched over your huge 750-page journal for months, I try to assemble the scattered pieces of your life, understand the reasons for your infatuations and disappointments, especially your frantic desire to connect with men, women (some loved with words, others with hands) before you ended up alone, destroyed, bitter, unrepentant, ready to begin again.

A love of love, a love of writing, your two sacraments, kept your head above water until Yelabuga and your encounter with the hill, the winding road, the potato field, the cypress.

Above all the cypress, viewed as a friend because it looked like a pencil, although it couldn't write or create shade when the August sun transformed the village into a furnace. A tree meant for cemeteries, the cypress of Yelabuga perhaps wandered off a bit to the edge of that field to be the last thing you saw when you closed your eyes.

You weren't made for that life.

Your aspirations were incompatible with the society around you and the country that had turned its back on the world and on the universe in which you had been raised.

Such an abrupt change; the October revolution imposed its law.

You had to learn how to live humbly, become invisible, not attract attention, expect at any moment to be denounced, arrested, deported, shot.

You had to grovel, though you were a rebel and continued to aspire to the absolute even when you begged from your friends, when your dresses wore out and dirty dishes piled up in the sink.

You would write as long as daylight shone on the page. You wrote feverishly; the sound of the pen on the paper, the only sound permitted between the walls that closed in as the daylight waned. Poems, translations, letters flowed in the disorder.

You stopped at nightfall when the oil lamp transformed a chair, an umbrella, some clothing hanging from a nail into ghosts. You called out to Alya, Irina, Sergei, to be sure they existed. You hallucinated, no longer knew why you were clutching a piece of bread in your hand or if the man you married at the age of 19 wasn't the product of your imagination.

Your parents' house transformed into communal apartments, and you, incapable of cohabitating with individuals who were enemies of the bourgeoisie to which you belonged, you moved outside the city, into a former concierge's apartment, far from the arguments that went on in what was once your parents' music room.

Women fought fiercely for a bar of soap, a pail of water when the toilet bowl became clogged.

Everything degenerated into fist-fights, insults constantly shouted, Kolkhoz dialects tangled together. Husbands called to the rescue fought, children screamed, wailed.

You mourned the destruction of your mother's piano, its ebony wood chopped into kindling for the fireplace, mourned the desk of your father, an art historian, the creator of the Moscow Fine Arts Museum, which a thug had taken for himself.

The notes your mother's fingers once played sang out over the years, wound into the poem you write, your eyes closed so not to frighten off the words. You write until your words and your strength are exhausted.

Emerging from anonymity with your first collection, the poet and literary critic Max Voloshin in the press praised the birth of a young poet.

Famous at the age of 17, publications opened their pages to you.

You say out loud what others dare not think.

'Max Voloshin saves the Whites from the Reds, and the Red from the White,' you dared say when silence would have been the better choice.

The giant who knocked on your parents' door wanted to meet Marina Tsvetaeva and hand her personally his impassioned hymn to female poetry and to the joy of being 17.

His 110 kilos crammed in between the arms of a chair, he asked you to change your hairstyle and take off your glasses.

'I can't see anything without my glasses.'

'You don't need to see. They just need to see you.'

You jabbered on, didn't agree with his admiration of Rimbaud, Baudelaire, Francis Jammes, Claudel, Mallarmé.

You preferred Rostand and German literature. Your bedside book: the life of *l'Aiglon*, the Eaglet, the son of Bonaparte, the sworn enemy of the Russian people.

Voloshin quickly understood that you were a renegade incapable of thinking like everyone else, incapable of adhering to a movement.

You amused him, whereas you wanted to attract his attention.

It was at his place in Koktebel in Crimea that you met the young Sergei Efron, whom you married one year later against the advice of your father who was never able to thwart your wishes. You imposed your will, imposed a poetry that had nothing in common with that of the poets who came before you.

You were fascinating, troubling. Frightening.

No empathy for the woman who writes things they have difficulty understanding.

Their inability to understand had no effect on you.

You wouldn't fail as long as you had a man in the world to love you. As long as your husband is alive whereas he is dead in the nightmare that awakened you yesterday. Sergei's soul was floating in the air, beating against the ceiling as if to break through before drifting away.

Wed before the revolution, he gave you two children before joining the White Army, leaving you alone to fight against the poverty and ruling regime who saw you as the wife of a traitor, an enemy of the Communists.

'Come back and I'll love you like a dog,' you begged him in a letter that he perhaps never received.

Others took his place while you awaited his return. Loves without futures. Actors in a theater that you frequented and which suited your bohemian spirit.

You 'unwound' to pass the time leading up to Sergei Efron's return, but always returned to your writing, like a goat to its stake.

Dying, I'll not say: 'I was'.

No regrets, I'll not cast blame.

There are greater things in this world

Than love's storm, and passion's game.

But you—wing-beat against my chest,

Fresh, guilty cause of my inspiration—

You I command to:—Be!

My obedience—knows no evasion.

30 June 1918

Surrounded by enemies and friends, and yet so alone with Alya whom you had to feed so she would escape the fate of Irina whose death you hid out of shame. So you wouldn't feel guilty. Solitude: the real cause of your tragic end.

The appearance of a man at your door one night put an end to your passing infatuations and to your distress.

Vyacheslav Ivanov, poet and great theoretician of symbolism, was knocking at your door.

'May I come in?'

A shocked look at the tattered sofa, the rickety chairs, the dusty floor, the dirty dishes.

Alya, who never missed anything, explains that her mother washes the inside of the plates. Only the inside.

'Mama is a poet.'

'How can you live in this squalor?'

'We sleep outside when it's really messy.'

'You never sweep up?'

'The roaches do that.'

'It's terrible! You must need many things.'

'We don't need anything except papa.'

Alya had an answer for everything.

Vyacheslav in your home. You couldn't believe your eyes.

'I'll take you to Florence.'

Your heart had stopped beating. You could have kissed his hand.

It didn't matter that he didn't keep his promise. A man was holding out his hand. You had to take it, place it on your breasts, your belly, he had to wring you out, he had to soothe your incandescent skin.

He promised to return. Maybe he would love you.

'An unloved body is a coffin,' you wrote in your notebook after he left.

Nothing but passions in such a small body. Your thinness was frightening. You did without so Alya could eat. When one has lost one child to hunger, one believes the other will never eat enough.

Vyacheslav wasn't the only one who knocked on your door. Rare were the days when you didn't have a visitor. Poets, painters, actors, or friends arrived at any time of the day or night. They came to compare their dire situations with yours, to discover that there were those who were needier than they. There was even a pawn broker, every object saved from your father's house exchanged for food.

Tobacco for grain, your father's lovely bronze inkwell for some red ink, his tiger eye snuffbox for a ream of paper, your mother's jewellery box for a silk suit, necessary ever since you took a new lover.

There was even a process server; the water leak that had done enormous damage to the apartment below became a mere drip without consequences when you offered to draft the charges for him.

Ready for everything in order to be loved, even to translate the work of the devil if you were asked to.

Hadn't you rewritten the journal of Prince Wolkonsky, without previously having met him, without being remunerated? Rewritten by hand to thank him for having offered to house you and your family in his palace in Crimea to escape the civil war in Moscow.

Your daughters entrusted to your sister-in-law, you made the voyage alone with a stop in Koktebel to bring your sister Assia, who had fallen into great poverty after the death of her husband, and her baby back to Moscow.

A trip that was true folly. The Bolshevik army blocked all the roads. They arrested people for any reason at all. Every citizen was considered suspicious. Arrested, shot, without a trial. Intellectuals first. Akhmatova interrogated, watched closely, her husband Nikolay Gumilyov executed, Sergei Yesenin shot. Alexander Blok dead under mysterious circumstances. Vladimir

Mayakovsky shot himself in the head, Mandelstam's body thrown into a common grave. Forbidden from writing, forbidden from earning a living, he died insane in the Vladivostok camp for having written:

> *All we hear is the Kremlin mountaineer,*
> *The murderer and peasant-slayer.*

Only official poets lived well. Headquartered in the Rostov palace, the powerful Writers' Union distributed apartments, dachas, and cars to friends of the regime. Pasternak enjoyed residing in the beautiful dacha-complex of Peredelkino. The receptions hosted by Ilya Ehrenburg in his lavish apartment on Gorky Street were just as sumptuous as those of the former bourgeoisie. Servers in starched headpieces served champagne and caviar canapés to guests, on the walls hung paintings by Vlaminck, Cezanne, Manet.

You were among the reprobates who shared an apartment, a stove, a toilet. You roamed the streets looking for a pair of boots, a sack of rice, some coal.

Endless lines in front of empty shops. Waiting for new shipments could last one or two days. Those who slept rough in the queue shared the sidewalk with new beggars from the recently impoverished middle class.

Eager to fight alongside the Whites, Sergei joined the rebel army leaving you alone with your two daughters. Alone and destitute, you could call upon no one. No more mail since the rebel groups had divided up the country, and no more news of Sergei.

Thinking of him did not improve your everyday life. This poem
is an illustration.

> I am come in the depth of night, and face you,
> My last hope of rescue.
> Kinsfolk forgotten, I wander, floundering,
> A ship foundering.
> [. . .]
> Impostors, like wolves, have hounded me,
> Utterly plundered me.
> Before your palace, true tsar and only one,
> I stand—lowly one!

27 April 1916

Wearing a fur chapka hat, very distinguished, Prince Wolkonsky who burst into your domestic chaos can't believe that the poet praised in the press can be this frail and so-badly-dressed young woman.

He is enthralled. You are fascinated.

A ghost from the time of the tzars is standing at your door.

The fact that he is homosexual and you're a false widow reassures you.

That he kisses your hand ravaged by household chores raises you up in your own self-esteem.

You are no longer beneath contempt.

The sides of his long coat held up, His Highness sits in the only armchair that isn't broken.

There follows a long friendship built on understanding and tenderness. Ambiguous loves, equivocal friendships would always be part of your life.

'I loved the prince who wasn't attracted to women,' you would write years later to the critic Bakhrakh. 'I loved him until he fell completely under my power. It is the obstinacy of love that allowed me to conquer him. He never learned to love women, but he learned to love love.'

The prince would support you even if your poetry didn't move him, even though the police were keeping an eye on you, even after the savage searches of your home and your writing, despite the annoyances and the interrogations you endured, your head held high.

An interminable winter, days so short, endless nights. You sweep, scrub, wash, but it's never clean enough. You cut up wood that never produces enough heat, peel potatoes without ever sating your daughter's hunger.

Unhappy with your life, you write, even in your sleep, and you awaken as exhausted as a field worked by a rusty harrow.

Writing, your revenge for the premature death of your mother.

Her career as a pianist interrupted, you swore you would pursue yours even if the times weren't right.

The poems that fell from your pen ended up in a drawer. Forgotten, as long as the civil war prevented their publication. Filed away in the same drawer as Irina who travels through your memory without lingering; your thoughts reserved for Alya who gets thinner every day. It's out of the question to place her in another institution where she might be better fed; the sad end of Irina taught you a lesson.

You prefer to keep her with you, even if it means watching her waste away.

'I am toxic for my daughter, being separated from her would thus be the only solution.'

Your affair with Vyacheslav prevents you from sinking.

Without a sturdy shoulder to lean on, you focus on writing. Writing lifts you above a sordid everyday life. Forgotten, the war and the lack of news from Sergei, you line up your words while others are getting themselves killed.

In your rat hole you receive poets, painters, and great minds with the grace of a lady.

You shine among all these men. Only the uncertainty about the fate of your husband preoccupies you. Having lovers doesn't prevent you from still thinking about him, from loving him more since you think he might be dead.

He has been gone for three years.

Short-lived consolations, your affairs with younger men, women, too; among them the poet Sophia Parnok who takes you, rejects you, because she can't desire a woman who has given birth.

Fleeting infatuations. Many loved you, but no one killed himself for you.

'Sophia Parnok trampled on me, but I always got back up,' you wrote in your journal.

Seeing that she only had eyes for a young woman poet during an evening of poetry-reading, you shouted over everyone's heads:

'I love you Sophia, even if you have bad taste, and I will continue to love you like a dog.'

Your blood is too hot, you seek pleasure for pleasure's sake, your remedy against your desperate life.

Being slapped doesn't discourage you. You laugh as if it is just a good joke, pride yourself for enduring, then begin again.

You tell about your troubles to anyone who will listen, every shoulder is good to cry on.

Nothing but infatuations, break-ups, and poems written in three years.

They ended up in the same drawer, with Irina; you struck the air above your shoulder when the little dead girl fluttered into your thoughts.

There's no room for empathy. The times didn't permit it. There were more urgent things to do: Send Alya away to school where she would get enough to eat, and find out if your husband is still alive, and if not, in what ground he is buried.

Eager to go away to school, Alya forgets to kiss you.

Christmas without Sergei, without children, without church bells, without turkey, without a cake, isn't Christmas.

You're alone. The sudden darkness between your walls pushes you outside. The streetlights are welcoming companions and the scrawny fir tree that no one wanted, a friend.

You drag it home, decorate it with what you have at hand. Three candles and three ribbons brighten it up.

Another Christmas and in other times, Alya had compared the tree to a dancer.

'A dancer yourself,' you mumble to the prematurely aged woman in the mirror alone in front of you. Grey hairs poking through, eyes sunken in their sockets, a bitter mouth and a threadbare dress.

A dancer because you dance on a volcano since you don't know what tomorrow will bring.

Wife of a traitor to the revolution, daughter of a friend of the tsar, a friend who founded the Fine Arts Museum, you could go to prison, be deported. Let them shoot you.

The tsar's letter of condolence when your mother died made you an enemy of the revolution. Hidden in your pillow, the letter takes you back to her slow death.

The family standing around her bed holding their breath. A father widowed for the second time, his two wives taken by the same illness: tuberculosis. Four children and four obligatory kisses on the frozen forehead of the dying woman.

It was Christmas then, too. Tears of rain on the windows, followed by thick snow that hid everything from view.

An impression of being alone in the world with the woman who continued to die. Alone with the large, twinkling tree in the entrance of the big house.

Irina died far away from you, ten years later as Christmas was coming. Before? After?

You don't try to find out.

No more trees within your walls. You drag yours outside.

You trample it with both feet. From afar, you seem to be dancing. A dancer yourself, a cursed dancer.

Rid of the tree harbinger of bad luck, you enjoy wondering what your fate would have been if you hadn't married Sergei Efron.

You would have tied the knot with your first love, Pyotr Ivanovich, the brother of Sonia, your classmate, loved the summer in Tarusa, forgotten the autumn in Moscow. Or five years later you might have become the mistress of Max Voloshin who sang the praises of your second collection *The Magic Lantern*, introduced you to a large audience, then invited you to read your poems in upscale circles.

You were 17—30 years and 60 kilos separated you from him. You weighed 40 kilos, he, 120. You were 150 centimetres tall, he, a meter 10. The bear and the doll.

Without Sergei Efron in your life, you might have married the poets Lvovich or Lann. You would have been the official mistress of Sophia Parnok who rejected you because you had a husband, children, because you had given birth, nursed, had become a mammal instead of a goddess.

Love, the only remedy for your fear of the Cheka and its spies, for your sordid existence: the floor and the laundry to wash, wood to find, the strength to blow on reluctant embers when you were out of breath. Breath reserved for your poems.

Your destiny would have been more spectacular if you had shared the life of Prince Wolkonsky in his palace in Crimea not yet touched by the revolution. His homosexuality, your free spirit, were made for you to get along. Your life would certainly have been less difficult if you had married Ehrenburg or Andrei Biely, but more tragic if you had married Mandelstam who loved you unrequitedly. You seduced him during a gathering in Petersburg, then rejected him in Moscow where he came to meet you.

You could maintain ten affairs that were physical or through correspondence at the same time, making each person believe he or she was the only one.

How many hours spent writing to reproach Ilya Ehrenburg for his lack of understanding, his intransigence, and for making light of everything.

One doesn't like one's wounds, one doesn't become giddy over one's wounds. One wants to heal or die. To love one's pain because it is pain that is against nature . . .

So many letters exchanged, one need only read between the lines to understand that Ilya Ehrenburg was jealous of Andrei Biely whom you were consoling during his separation from his wife, the widow of Alexander Blok, who died from neglect by order of Stalin.

You wanted to be Messalina, whereas you had neither the physique nor the means. Empress of the gutters, your court was a gaggle of poets as wretched as you. Despite the splendour of your poems your two-room apartment was not Byzantium.

You and Ehrenburg crossed swords at the slightest provocation. Bitter-sweet his commentary on the great soiree of Russian women poets organized by Bryusov in the auditorium of the Polytechnic Museum:

> Prideful attitude, high forehead, short hair, the face of an impudent urchin, Marina Tsvetaeva glorifies in fiery pathos an insolence worthy of the greatest heretics, philosophers, or rebels. Her excellent verses will remain as will her thirst for living and for destroying everything. The struggle of one person against all and the love glorified by the death waiting in the wings . . .

Love, the theme of the evening, good for the other poets, not for you. Your poem 'Swans,' an impassioned homage to the White Army, had shaken your audience. You had deviated from the rule, disobeyed Bryusov, managed to shock. You were asked for a love poem, you gave them a war poem.

You remained on the side of the defeated whereas Ehrenburg who thought mainly of his career remained on the side of the conquerors.

You opened your arms to him out of great necessity, used him like the others to make your separation from your husband less wrenching.

A poem describes this:

I wrote it on a blackboard of dark slate,
Along the tiny folds of faded fans,
Along a river's sands, on the seashore,
With skates on ice, using my ring on glass . . .
On treetrunks living a centennial winter
And, finally, so everyone can know
How constantly, unfailingly I love you,
Added my name, a rainbow, on the sky.

18 May 1920

A great poet, a great lover, a great talker.

You loved and hated with the same passion, your soul white-hot. There was a volcano in you.

Burn down, destroy to rebuild according to your criteria, life inconceivable if it isn't transfigured.

You felt confined in a society that had given up, confined among poets who glorified the regime, confined in your country. You quarrelled with your neighbours, couldn't stand the close quarters, didn't respond to their greetings.

Your apartment cluttered with useless objects, your garbage pail enthroned on your landing, you wanted to displease, make enemies. You fought in order to free the howling held prisoner in your chest.

Spiteful, wearing old rags, a silver ring on each finger, you welcomed with sarcasm anything that didn't align with your convictions.

It was time for you to leave the country, join your husband, the father of Alya and Irina whose death he didn't know about, find the one who had been gone for three years, even if it meant searching the entire continent. Including under the ground.

Curiously, it was Ehrenburg himself who would arrange everything to help you find Sergei Efron who had disappeared into thin air since the defeat of the monarchists and their scattering over the continent.

A thorough investigation carried out in the Kremlin, where he had connections, led him to Prague. The former officer had been living there as a student since the defeat of the White Army.

Czechoslovakia at the time welcomed all Russian migrants who flowed into its territory, issued grants to students, and housed them while waiting for them to earn a living.

You learned the news of Sergei's resurrection from Pasternak whom you didn't know at the time, good news conveyed by a future lover. Ehrenburg who no longer wanted your love owed you that as compensation.

Pasternak, from that time indissociable from your entire existence. Living apart, each on a continent, each married, you nourished a correspondence that spanned a quarter century. With his bad marriage at the time, you considered him single, which was no longer the case ten years later after he met Zinaida Nikolaevna.

You and Zinaida had nothing in common. She loved everything you abhorred. Zinaida had curtains on her windows, rugs on the floors of her apartment, a refrigerator in her kitchen, a son whom she was raising in the cult of Stalin, while you had only your words and instilled in Alya a hatred of Bolsheviks.

Although married, Boris Pasternak belonged to you; the distance between you didn't keep you from continuing to love him.

To Boris Pasternak

Dis-tances: miles, versts . . .
We're dis-severed, dis-persed,
They've rendered us silent, terse,
At the far ends of the earth.
Distances: tracts, versts . . .
We're disjointed, and disbursed,
Displayed, splayed, un-destroyed,
They don't know we're . . . an alloy

24 March 1925

A philology student at the University of Prague, Sergei was entitled to a grant that allowed him just enough to get by. Joining him there became your obsession. The family needed to be reunited under the same roof again, Alya needed to be reacquainted with the father whose face she had forgotten.

But what words could you use to tell him about the death of Irina, your battle to save an ill Alya, your endless struggle against wretchedness?

And how could you get a visa to leave the country when you were on the wrong side of the regime?

You owed the passport delivered by the authorities to Ehrenburg, to the tragic death of Irina, and to the fact that you didn't belong to a party.

'Take the train to Berlin in three days. My wife and I will meet you at the station. We've reserved a room for you in our hotel. Travel light so you won't attract attention,' he had recommended.

You're glad to leave, but troubled by the heap of objects to sort through.

What should you keep, what should you leave behind?

Sitting on the cold floor, you and Alya make two piles.

Leave: the copper basin, the old samovar, the chipped plates, the threadbare rug. Leave: the photos, immediately burned in the fireplace. You give the red silk shawl to your neighbour, a woman of ill-repute, whom you know only by her white arms as she closes the shutters whenever a client arrives; your mother's shawl would cover her nakedness if by accident two appointments overlapped.

But a ball presents a problem. To whom should you leave it now that its owner is gone? A rubber ball like any other ball. You kept it out of superstition because of a dream. You were digging in the ground looking for it to return it to Irina. Digging a hole deeper and deeper, into another hole, as far as Hell, if necessary, but you found nothing. The feeling of guilt had continued after you awakened. Irina was already dead but you didn't know; the orphanage had forgotten to tell you.

Thirty years of life reduced to two suitcases: after the essentials you add your mother's incense burner, Irina's ball, and the family icon.

You make the sign of the cross.

Alya does the same.

You love God ever since the Bolsheviks kicked him out of the country.

Three days and three nights on the train with stops in gloomy stations. You close your eyes so you won't see the landscapes that rush by out the window. The houses are tombs, cities cemeteries, valleys chasms, and forest trees, conspirators. You open your eyes only to make sure your manuscripts are still there.

Looking at the land of your misery is too painful.

Overjoyed at the idea of seeing her father again, Alya finds the journey interminable. You sleep. Bizarre, that dream when the train has just crossed over the Iron Curtain.

You're in the same train, but surrounded by thick fog. You are dead, but don't know it yet. Men coming out of nowhere lean over you. They are naked but you are clothed. They talk about you without using your name as if they didn't know you. You recognize them by their voices. Ilya Ehrenburg, Yevgeny Lann, Boris Pasternak, Andrei Biely, Vyacheslav, even Rilke whom you never met, but with whom you correspond thanks to Pasternak.

Gathered together for the first time in the same place, they appear to be getting along, to have the same objective.

From their confabulations you understand that they are to undress you to make you presentable. The word 'presentable' is uttered by all.

Coat, dress, undergarments are taken off in the blink of an eye, they divide the space on your skin among themselves. 'To each his page and no more than two lines,' says the one who seems to be leading the operation. Pens are moving over your body, scratching out sentences that you know, since you wrote them.

'I write with rage, dear Ilya. That is my life, the word obviously likes me a lot. But I can't stop betraying it in favour of humans who have never ceased to reject me . . .'

'Happy to death, dear Nikolay, to have seen you yesterday in my house where everything is broken, for listening to me talk about my inability to adapt to life, for making me believe that I can still be loved.'

'You are greater than your poems, dear Yevgeny Lann, greater in my life.'

'Your longing for me, Boris, resembles that of Adam for Lilith. You are automatically condemned. Even if I lose something in your eyes. Men have been charmed by me, never in love. That is my destiny.'

'Love hates the poet, dear Rilke, love doesn't want to be magnified. It is humble.'

'Now, in the time of conclusions, you have let go of my hand, Boris, to let me be stricken from the family of humans face to face with my humanity.'

The ink of their sentences having dried on your skin, they are enveloped by the same fog. Disappear as if by magic.

In a corner of the train car your husband is standing. Sergei obviously witnessed the scene without feeling the need to intervene. His face expressionless, not angry, not jealous. A feeling of compassion. Your Seryozha feels sorry for you.

The cold jerks you awake. The same piercing cold you felt when you learned of the deaths of Gumilyov and Yesenin, both executed, of the suicide of Mayakovsky, a bullet in his heart, of the untreated ill health and death of Alexander Blok, of the silence of Rilke who no longer answered your letters. Blinded by your passion for the author of *Orchards*, you didn't want to admit that he loved Lou Andreas-Salomé, that he was dying, that he loved your poetry, but not your person.

The words written on your skin float in the air of the train car. You recognize your writing. Recognize your clothing scattered around you.

You're ashamed to be naked though you are clothed, ashamed to still be alive. Ashamed of the way your husband looked at you, the only one not to have written even one sentence from the passionate letters you wrote him. The last one goes back two years:

12 March 1921

My Seryozha,

If you are alive, I am saved. We have been separated for three years. Alya is eight now. Writing to you frightens me. I've been living for so long in constant terror, not daring to hope you are alive, and from my forehead, my hands, my chest, I push away the other possibility. If God expects submission from me, I do so humbly. If you are alive, Seryozha, we will see each other again, we will have a son . . . If you are no longer, it would be better if I had never been born. I will write no more. I am already entirely inside you, so much that I no longer have eyes, lips, nor hands, nothing but breath and the beating of my heart.

Marina

Ilya Ehrenburg and his wife meet you at the station and take you to the hotel after inviting you to a restaurant.

Ilya works hard to obtain an exit visa from Czechoslovakia for Sergei who is eager to see his wife and daughters (he doesn't know about Irina).

Three years have passed since the departure of the former officer of the White Army now a student again, does he still love you and will he desire the woman you have become? So much anxiety before seeing him again.

The mirror shows you an old woman of 30. Shadows under your eyes. Grey hairs sticking out. It has snowed on your head, snowed in your heart.

You go to the cafes frequented by Russian emigres to pass the time that separates you from your husband. Discussions degenerate into disputes between individuals who are nonetheless on the same side.

Reconciled by the death of Lenin, they await the death of Stalin to shout victory and go home. Rumourmongers, gossipers, or sincerely concerned about the fate of their brothers, they want to know what has become of the exiled Bunin who fled Russia almost three months earlier. Some say he went to Sofia, others Constantinople, others Paris. That it is highly likely he'll be awarded the Nobel Prize.

Someone remembers having run into him at the Writers Union, sceptical in front of the statue of Pushkin.

'I will replace him one day on that pedestal,' he had confidently said.

An old man says he ran into Gorky on the arm of his wife in a street in Petersburg, but doesn't remember when.

'Does anyone know if Andrei Biely was able to convince his wife to come back to him?' wonders another.

Lips turned down. No one seems to know.

'Being the widow of Alexander Blok drove that poor Vera mad. She will be a widow for life.'

'She shouldn't have married Andrei. She made her own bed.'

'He'll end up consoling himself one day. Which isn't true of Nadezhda Mandelstam. Her husband buried in a common grave in Vladivostok, she couldn't retrieve his body. She wanders from town to town for fear of being caught by Stalin and meeting the same fate as her man.'

'That woman is a heroine. Forbidden to write, Osip dictated his poems to her, which she hid with loyal friends, in a pillow, a boot, a crack in the wall. Nadezhda begged from friends to feed him. Hunger forced them into the street on nights of heavy snow. They watched people through restaurant windows and tried to guess what they were eating:

' "The man on the right has an orange on his plate."

' " . . . orange peels," he corrected her.

' "The one in front of us is eating cheese."

' "You mean snow, which you have under your feet." '

You listen to them without hearing, hunched over your note-books which you bring with you like a cat its latest litter. A stranger everywhere except in your sheets of paper. A stranger to the misfortune of Mandelstam who loved you unrequitedly. You and Mandelstam were the same age, had the same desire to be famous. An anonymous dead man whereas your celebrity crossed borders. You are a myth for those who know your poetry; as well known as Akhmatova, but more modern. You are prolific whereas Anna forbade herself from writing so not to dis-please the regime that executed her husband Gumilyov and deported her son.

People admire your writing, not you. The years of misery have made you bitter. You want to shock the intellectuals, scan-dalize those who fled Russia at the first gunshot, provoke for the pleasure of provoking, dismay those who haven't shared your misfortune. Those whose children didn't die from neglect and hunger.

During a gathering in the hotel room of Khodasevich and Nina Berberova, with Andrei Biely and Ehrenburg, turning your nose up at those present, you tell them that aside from yourself, there will be no one left in Russian poetry.

Seeing their pursed mouths, you go even further in your provocation, unplug the lamp and use the sudden darkness to jump on Nina Berberova and kiss her on the mouth.

Nina, offended, pushes you away, her cries of a startled vir-gin double you over with laughter. You leave the room happy to have shocked them, made them angry. You maintain and refine your sour persona. 'The bourgeoisie doesn't know how to love,' you say to them before banging the door behind you.

Calling three great writers bourgeois, you've crossed a line.

You exude rebellion with your bohemian dresses, your silver rings on every finger and that candid and perverse way you look at men. Your convictions are upsetting. A hippy before the time of hippies.

Enchanting, that's how you describe your encounter with your Berlin publisher, the young Abraham Vichniak. He has been under your spell since you appeared in his office.

Your flouncy dress, your rings, your smoker's voice, everything bourgeois society rejects seduces the young director of Helikon Editions, ten years younger than you.

You sign all the contracts he offers: a translation of the new *Florentine Nights*, a long poem by Heine, the publication of your collection *Separation*, a translation into German of the latest collection by Alexander Blok. And why not your journal of the dark years in Moscow?

Vichniak would reconcile you with life. That man has been waiting for you forever. You are made for each other. You are indivisible.

Your imagination dictates this letter to you the evening following your meeting.

You liberate my female self in me, my most shadowy, most hidden self.

To the contracts signed in the morning in his Berlin office, you respond with a love letter, followed by others, one every day. You anxiously await a response, despair because he is late in responding, then are depressed when your letters are returned to you.

Vichniak wants you in his publishing catalogue, not in his bed.

A slap in the face, the returned letters. You fold into yourself, lick your wounds while preparing your revenge. One doesn't get away with humiliating Tsvetaeva. You will meet Vichniak four years later, on 13 January 1926 in Paris during an event at the Hotel Lutetia where rich expats are celebrating the Russian New Year. You will pretend not to recognize him, your lapse attributed to the fact that he no longer has a moustache or glasses whereas he never had a moustache or glasses.

An account of the incident would appear years later in your preface to the work that brought together all your love letters, without the name of the dedicatee ever being mentioned.

My complete lapse of memory and lack of recognition today are only your absolute presence and my complete absorption of yesterday. To the extent that you were, so are you no longer. Absolute presence in reverse . . . Such a presence can only become such absence. Everything— yesterday, nothing— today.

Signed Marina, with a furious pen.

To fall in love while your husband is languishing in Prague waiting for an exit visa to meet you doesn't seem at all immoral to you. Too many passions boil up in you. Impossible to reserve them for only one person.

Your dream: to gather around you all those who admire and love you. Whether lovers or friends, men or women, you want to live intensely. You dream of tumultuous scenes followed by ardent reconciliations bathed in tears of remorse.

Vichniak dismissed, you set your amorous sights on the poet and great scholar Marc Slonim; his glowing review of *Separation* sets your heart on fire. He lives in Prague, one more reason to move to that city where your husband lives.

Sergei obtains permission to leave Czechoslovakia, but you forget the hour of his arrival and reach the train station late. The train has already departed. You and Alya are dismayed and then you hear your name shouted out from another platform:

'Marina, Marinochka!'

You're in each other's arms. You embrace, you dry each other's tears, Sergei pays no attention to his daughter, he sees only you, looks only at you.

Alya looks at this father whose face she had forgotten and who seems younger than you. Nothing escapes her.

'At 28, my father looks like an adolescent,' she notes in her journal. 'He looks at Marina as an orphan would . . . '

An unheard-of expense given your means, the bottle of champagne uncorked that evening in your hotel room, but you were determined to celebrate the event. Little Irina is in everyone's thoughts. But no one speaks of her. To bring up her tragic end through hunger and neglect would ruin the mood. You have decided to turn the page. To live differently, to stifle your love for Pasternak. Learning of his imminent arrival in Berlin, you hasten your departure for Czechoslovakia. Meeting him risks destabilizing your marriage. You make do with his letters. Your love doesn't need his presence, it will survive the separation, even his anger when years later he would reproach you for having excluded him from the three-way correspondence with Rilke, a correspondence made possible through his connection to Rilke, and for your impassioned letters to Rilke. He's the one who had put you in contact with the author of *Orchards*, it was he who had initiated the correspondence between the three of you.

Pasternak had advised you to stop bothering Rilke who was battling leukaemia and was dying.

Ehrenburg had used the same word to discourage your impassioned letters to Vichniak.

Suddenly, Berlin has become hostile to you. You've made plenty of enemies in three weeks. It's a good thing you're following Sergei to Prague. Become a wife and mother again.

To write, above all to write.

You flee the man Pasternak but read and reread his poems through your tears, and write an essay on his collection:

My sister life.

. . . the mountain is complete in Pasternak. He is felt like the Urals, has become the Urals. He is transmutation of the object in self, its dissolution in self. All the rocks of the Urals are dissolved in his lyric flow . . .

In Pasternak the man speaks the language of mountains . . .

Pasternak responds to your praise with reproaches: why did you leave Berlin when he was coming to see you?

You begin writing to each other again, your letters cross the Iron Curtain after he returns to Russia for good, his letters would follow you to all the places you moved: from Berlin to Prague, to Mokropsy, to Všenory, to Moravská Třebová, then to Paris, before stopping abruptly the day after you returned to Russia, after your five-minute encounter on a subway platform in Moscow. He constantly looked at his watch. Zinaida was waiting for him . . .

Your last encounter, you hanged yourself soon afterwards.

With rents too high in Prague and your husband living in a barracks, you move to a town 30 minutes from the capital.

In her journal Alya writes of a forest, a village, log huts scattered in the wooded area, and a church that had kept its bell tower unlike those in Russia, where bells were melted down for economic or strategic reasons.

Sweet, the evenings with the three of you around the table cleared after supper. Sergei reads passages from the books he has brought from Prague, you and Alya listen to him while mending, sewing.

Alya admires his kindness and intelligence. You pretend to be happy. You sleep badly at night. You cry out in your sleep. You feel trapped in the village, in your life, in your skin.

Your contempt for household chores makes you flee the house. Alya does what she can not to arouse your anger. You know each tree in the neighbouring forest, you talk to them like friends. You would suffocate without your trips to Prague where you meet Marc Slonim who praised your last collection in the *Russian Gazette*.

A hothead like you, young Slonim. You complete each other. Two excessive beings, brains and bodies boiling over. Living dangerously is your motto.

The dust rag and broom unworthy of your person, you run to Prague whenever you can, burst into the newspaper room, take Slonim from his office, follow him to the cafe Slavia, then into his attic room.

Your body sated, you go home to resume your written dialogue with Pasternak. The distance that separates you guarantees your love. He will always be first in your thoughts.

Pasternak is permanent, the others are only fleeting.

Pages covered with your ardent writing, you feel at peace with yourself, with your husband who is gone from morning to evening.

Peace in your soul, superior to that of your love-making with Slonim.

Returning home from your lover, the house seems less dirty to you, the shortening days less sad, your dresses less old-fashioned.

When night falls, your husband's steps on the gravel path warm your heart. You are happy to see him back again whereas he has every reason to leave you. A goat attached to its stake, Sergei returns to the wife who cheats on him while swearing she loves him. His silences and closed face fill you with guilt. You try to cheer him by telling him of your projects, knowing how he loves and unwaveringly admires your writing.

Each of you has your life, his at the university where he goes every morning, you with your notebooks and lovers whom you meet physically or virtually through your correspondence.

He knows, but doesn't dare say anything, makes do with smelling the scent of the unknown male on your clothes. Moved by a surge of pride, the former officer of the White Army sometimes tries to put an end to his martyrdom. Divorce. His great goodness, his great kindness winning him over, he leaves you only in his thoughts. Separating from you means abandoning you to your inner demons, to your destructive tendencies, to your uncontrollable impulses.

With the same sadness Sergei breathes in the scent of your dresses and your letters to Pasternak which you neglect to seal. Asked to mail them, he sometimes reads a few lines, imagining that the impassioned words are addressed to him. That Marina is talking to him.

> Your voice for me is a burning. I'm burning from my head to my feet as if intimately caressed. To see you would have certainly delivered me from you, inside you, thereby satisfied . . .

Knowing that he always loves what you love, Sergei makes your veneration of Pasternak his own.

'Sergei Efron is Marina's double,' Andrei Biely would say.

Pasternak, your fire brother. Approaching him threatened to ignite you, to reduce you to ashes. Use any pretext not to meet him in Berlin before his final return to Russia. You mention a lack of money, the difficulty of obtaining an exit visa and leaving your family.

'Every tree my eyes will admire will be you,' you wrote to him before the country locked the door behind him for many long years.

'The moon is only beautiful when seen from afar,' was a saying.

Driven by your emotion, you contradicted yourself the next day though he had already left.

A request Pasternak:

Don't go to Russia without seeing me . . . To me, Russia is *un grand peut-être*, almost the beyond. If you left for Guadeloupe, snakes, lepers: I wouldn't summon you . . .

You already disappeared once—at the Novodevichy cemetery: you *removed* yourself, you simply were no longer there. Remembering that, I get scared—and I'm fighting for: what? Just a handshake . . .

I could write a book about our meetings, just resurrecting them, *without* invention . . .

Boris—*a wound for life*.

I don't fear your leaving but your disappearing.

Marina

You dread the disappearance of your husband humiliated by your endless affairs. Sergei abandons you in his thoughts as he stands in front of the map of Russia hanging on the wall. His pencil has drawn a winding line going from Prague to the White Sea. With false papers, he would go, leave you to your interchangeable lovers, to your relentless pen.

He does the dishes while you blacken the pages. Scrub, wash, dry, without making a sound. Sobs mutely behind the thin wall that separates the rooms.

'Seryozha is crying,' Alya tells you.

He should beat up his rival instead of snivelling, you think to yourself. A cockfight to win your heart wouldn't displease you.

Alya doesn't have the words to console her father.

If she had the means Alya would kill Pasternak who prevents her mother from being a wife and mother, would kill Slonim who makes her run every day to the station to the train that takes her to Prague.

Outside the night has taken hold of the dacha standing in the middle of the forest. Everything is silent. The trees are holding their breath. Only the sound of your pen on the page is heard. Is it to break this silence that Sergei in a neutral voice announces Alya's imminent departure to a boarding school?

Not daring to meet your eyes, he plunges his into the map of Europe tacked on the wall.

With his finger he traces the meandering borders, then the networks that connect cities. Sergei is looking for an unknown place where he can seek refuge far from the KGB which hasn't stopped hunting him, far from you, his living reproach. His finger moves around cities looking for hamlets without train stations. You watch the index finger which should move to the north, not to the south where the KGB would easily find him.

Why Tatary and that hamlet of Yelabuga which you see for the first time?

Yelabuga? A place you will never see, you say to yourself; the world is so big, much too big for a single life.

To return to Soviet land when he could seek refuge in one of the fiords of Iceland or Norway is madness.

Does he believe he can become invisible by throwing himself into the mouth of the wolf?

Childishness, you say to yourself and dive back into your page. Sergei will never leave you. You need his presence to confirm your power over him.

The word invisible written that same evening addressed to Pasternak.

O, along which seas and cities to search for you!
(Invisible one—sought by a blind woman!)
I entrust my farewells to the wires,
And leaning against a telegraph pole I cry.

You love that which escapes you and explain yourself in your journal:

I have loved everything in my life in the form of adieu not of meeting, of rupture, not of fusion.

You broke ties with all your friends in Berlin whom you called intellectuals, cold aesthetes, their sensibilities replaced with commonplaces, your forgotten companions of the dark years.

You write to none of those who knocked on your Moscow door day and night. You opened it without the slightest hesitation. Nothing to steal at your place or anyone else's. The same destitution everywhere. Hunger caused insomnia. What seemed like ghosts were only emaciated men. They walked to forget their hunger, with the hope of running into someone hungrier than they.

Three years of misery. An entire stretch of your life henceforth erased.

You now write only to Pasternak and to the young literary critic Alexander Bakhrakh who called your latest collection *Craft* a great event.

A gift from heaven that Bakhrakh. He would console you for the absence of Pasternak and the disappearance of Slonim who went off with another woman.

A bitter-sweet break up told in this poem:

What's it like with another woman—
Simpler?—a flash of the oar!—
[. . .]
What's life like with an *ordinary*
Woman? . . .
Without the divinity?

With Slonim in love elsewhere, you redirect your passion onto Bakhrakh, ten years younger than you, and write to him every day.

Your first letter: an erudite mixture of seduction and inter-pretation of your poetry.

A change of tone in your second: you veer off course and can't stop yourself from including your emotions.

I have so many words and so many feelings for you, my friend . . .

I don't know you but I have taken you into my life. I walk with you on the dusty path of the village and along the smoke-filled streets . . . a tiny mountain village, a simple izba, a well to get water at the bottom of the hill.

You tell him you're happy to learn that you're known and liked in Berlin.

That I am known and not liked, that's common; that I'm not known and liked—often.

Writing to Bakhrakh, to Pasternak, fills your days. Incapable of doing any housework since Alya left for boarding school, you convince Sergei to leave Mokropsy for a tiny apartment in a working-class town outside Prague.

A grim neighbourhood. Not a single tree in sight. The noise of carts and cars outside your window prevents you from writing. Having severed ties with all your friends from before, you have only one correspondent left: Bakhrakh whom you flood with your letters.

Seduced by the first ones, Bakhrakh is now smothered. You want to monopolize all his thoughts. You prevent him from working. All the time asking him for advice, giving him responsibilities:

—get you an exit visa out of Czechoslovakia;

—find you a place to stay during your next trip to Berlin for the release of your collection *Earthly Signs*;

—hire a charming young woman who likes your poetry to accompany you shopping;

—escort you to your publishers and to public places (entertainment and celebrations, you specify);

—help you choose a man's watch, reliable and inexpensive, for your Sergei;

—above all tell you if he has a family who views every woman as a *femme fatale*.

Then this P.S. of astonishing clarity:

'I will be coming for two weeks. Enough time to fight with old friends and make new enemies.'

Then:

'Don't mention in your letters what I've asked you, respond with action.'

Bakhrakh plays dead. Too heavy to bear. You overwhelm him. He needs to breathe.

He maintains his silence in spite of your moving letter describing the nature of your relationship.

> What do I lose by losing you? The temporary course of my soul, the common denominator of my acts and my days, my condition: once again flooded.
>
> You were the course of my river, my shape, my indispensable grip . . . my little tree. Soul and youth, an encounter of two absolutes. Could I have considered you a man? . . . I am a stripped person whereas you all wear armour. You all have art, life, society, friendships, distractions, family, duty, I, deep down, I have nothing. Everything falls like a skin and under the skin there is raw flesh . . . I can live only in dreams . . . die because of everything.

Strange conclusion:

> I'm not comforting you, I'm surprising myself. I cannot live and love here.

Signed Marina

Receiving no response to your letters, after a month you become depressed, and for the first time doubt your magnetic power. The same scenario as with Vichniak: rejected after being put on a pedestal. Scorned after being venerated.

Conclusion: neither Slonim nor Bakhrakh deserve you.

Your contempt for the two of them doesn't keep you from suffering.

Suddenly everything seems ugly: your two-room apartment over a cafe, the noisy street under your window. Your worn-out furniture, the two narrow windows. You look from the passers-by, the badly clothed workers, to the dirty dishes piled up in the sink.

You shouldn't have allowed Alya to go. Sending her to a boarding school was a bad idea.

You'll fix that.

Quickly throwing on your coat, you run to the train station without asking the father's opinion as if you had made her alone (Marina had impregnated Marina).

Passers-by turn around to stare at the dishevelled woman running and muttering unintelligibly.

You don't care. None of them know your poetry, not even one of your verses.

You are not in your normal state when, at the school, you ask Alya if she's happy there.

'Yes,' responds the 11-year-old girl. 'I have friends, it's fun.'

Her response freezes you. How can Alya be friends with these insipid little bourgeoises who will become idiotic and pretentious women?

You find suspicious the maniacal cleanliness of the place, the impeccable uniforms, the 'hello ma'am, thank you ma'am' and the forced smiles.

Soulless puppets. They will rub off on Alya.

You pull her out of the school despite her good grades and the director's insistence that she remain.

'Alya is a very good student, a precocious child . . .'

But you won't be swayed.

Her place is alongside you and nowhere else.

You don't speak to each other on the return journey. Alya forces herself not to cry, the drops of rain on the train window are the tears she's holding back.

Back home, the girl knows what awaits her. The broom, the mop stand ready for her. You have an opus to complete.

Your pen, your only connection to the world. Others have a duster.

You write to the young snob who didn't appreciate you, you turn things back to your advantage. The scales are tipped in your favour because the decision to break up is yours.

You advise him to be brave and listen to you.

Something is over between us. I'm in love with another, I can't say it more plainly or more truthfully. Have I ceased to love you? No. You haven't changed nor have I changed. Only one thing has changed: my sensory designs for you. You haven't ceased to exist for me, whereas I have ceased to exist for you. My hour with you has ended. There remains my eternity with you . . . Beyond passions, I'm not comforting you, I'm surprising myself. I cannot live and love here.

Signed Marina

You write to purge your shame, so not to choke on your own rage.

In the evening, after supper, only the scratching of your pen on paper can be heard. Your fierce writing coupled with the desire to destroy what you have just written. Alya and Sergei, powerless spectators of your self-destruction. They watch you racing to the abyss but do nothing to stop you. The involuntary tear that you believe you wiped from the corner of your eye dilutes a word in passing. No tenderness for yourself. The horror is behind you.

Behind you Irina buried in a shoebox, hunger in Moscow in the grip of civil war, fear of being denounced, arrested, shot, behind you dead bodies in the streets, the dust of bombings breathed in with the air. Dust that has travelled over borders, follows you wherever you go.

Alya sweeps, scrubs, washes without making any noise so not to disturb your inspiration.

Sunk in a chair, Sergei rocks back and forth like a praying rabbi, suggesting a resurfacing of his Jewish origins.

He disapproves of Alya's return, but doesn't dare say so. He suffers without a reproach escaping his mouth. He will divulge his grievances to Max Voloshin, the same Voloshin who once knocked at your door, 13 years ago, in your vacation house in Tarusa to give you his article praising your first poems, to advise that you take off your glasses and no longer square-cut your hair.

The giant, a meter ten tall, as many kilos in weight, took you under his wing for two reasons.

Primo you are a true poet. *Deuxio* you had lost your mother. A recognized poet at the age of 17, motherless at 13; your mother's grave in the village cemetery, a stone's throw from the house where the Tsvetaev family spent their summer vacations.

In his letter to Voloshin, Sergei talks of your blindness and of how difficult it is for him to leave you though you are at a dead end and your life in common has become infernal.

He describes you as a creature of passion, ready to throw yourself into fleeting romances; yesterday's affairs turned into tomorrow's derisions.

'I am in a fog,' he concludes in his letter to Voloshin,

I don't know what to do; Marina has become such an embedded part of me that now although I'm working on our separation, I am devastated, torn. I'm trying to live with my eyes closed so I won't see anything.

A spectator of your passions, Sergei who suffers to see you go from exaltation to disappointment has reluctantly decided to leave you.

A decision not kept in the face of your despair.

You no longer sleep, you're losing weight, cry day and night, and refuse to be separated from him.

'Knowing you're alone would leave me without a minute of peace,' you are persuaded that you are protecting him whereas you are slowly destroying him.

'I am both your life jacket and dead weight,' he responds.

To choose between Sergei and Konstantin, between your husband and your lover is beyond your strength. The two men are complementary and not at all incompatible.

To separate from one of the two takes you back to the dark years when you sacrificed Irina to save Alya from death.

Your Russian friends in Prague disapprove of your behaviour and praise the patience of your husband, so dignified in spite of his suffering.

Khodasevich, Nina Berberova, Andrei Biely, Ilya Ehrenburg feel sorry for him. Anxious to save your reputation, Sergei continues to accompany you in society, seems gracious when his heart isn't in it anymore.

Something unbelievable: it was among his close friends that you found your new lover. A former officer in the White Army, the handsome Konstantin Rodzevich was the close friend of Sergei Efron, his fellow traveller.

Mutual love at first sight. Nothing stops you. The suffering inflicted on your spouse and his friend don't matter. Impossible to fight against the tempest. Unleashed, you don't try to be discreet. You exhibit your passion in the streets, the cafes, you talk about it freely. You are blind to everything that isn't about you two. You meet every afternoon at your place when Sergei is running late at the university. Your lovemaking resembles wild rituals. You devour each other.

He wants to marry you but you hesitate. The gypsy fortuneteller to whom he takes you demolishes his plans. She sees you living on two different continents, tells you you'll have a life cut off from its other half like your lifeline that is stopped in the middle of your palm.

You listen to her without hearing, your gaze follows the wanderings of the cats in the tiny apartment. A large black cat is busy unrolling a ball of yarn, a small ginger one is licking the bottom of a coffee cup, a golden one drinks directly from the partially open sink tap. Sprawling in a filthy armchair, the one that seems to be the mother is taking a nap.

Never seen so many cats in so little space. Where does the Pythonissa sleep and why is she so eager to destroy your spirit?

Outside you can breathe again. He is sad and you're eager to return home. You're happy to give yourself to him during the day but insist on going back to Pasternak in his poems at night, find Akhmatova whom you recite when you can't sleep. Rodzevich soothes your body, Akhmatova your soul, and Pasternak your heart:

My sister—life—in a flood of spring rain
Has bruised herself blue all around us today,
But people in watches seem peevish and vain
And bite so politely, like vipers in hay.
The old have their motives for such goings on,
Your motives most likely are silly, I'll bet:
That eyes in a storm go all lilac like lawns,
The atmosphere heavy with moist mignonette.

You sip Akhmatova's poems with your cup of tea, wonder and sadness steeped in the same water.

Rain, dew, grass, and rivers of Pasternak complement the embraces of Rodzevich.

Love, your antidote against the three-year death experienced in Moscow.

You breathe deeply, now that your body is sated, are seen with the handsome man who has nothing in common with those who preceded him. Doesn't write, doesn't read, doesn't paint, is simply handsome and knows how to exalt your flesh.

You dedicate poems to him that you will give to others when your passion will have waned, you liken him to the knight whose statue is watching over the waters of the Danube.

Glorified, venerated, you will bring him down off his pedestal three months later, claiming he took advantage of your body without touching your soul.

Pregnant, you don't attempt to find out who your child's father is. Sergei Efron or Konstantin Rodzevich? It doesn't matter.

Rumours run wild in the expat circles whereas in your head, only your head, the father is none other than Pasternak, present in your notebooks. He impregnated you through writing, with his magic ink, over the Iron Curtain that closed behind him, under the noses of your husband and your lover both of whom claim to be the true father.

You give birth on February 1, at home and not in the hospital, in the midst of a snowstorm. Women, neighbours whom you scarcely know, bustle around you. It doesn't matter if the child didn't cry, you've given birth to a son. It takes 20 minutes to revive him. The activity around you doesn't concern you, you repeat, drunk with happiness: 'My son, my son'.

The child bathed, dressed, you decide to call him Boris.

A name adamantly rejected by your husband concerned with keeping up appearances.

'Boris as in Pasternak,' you repeat, deaf to the arguments of poor Sergei who searches among the names of all the orthodox saints for one that doesn't belong to one of your former lovers.

Rejected: Max, Marc, Andrei, Ilya, Boris, Dimitri, and others; he opts for Georgy. As far as he knows, you've never had an affair with a Georgy. He insists for personal reasons: Saint George who slew the dragon will be able to crush his wife's demons.

You circumvent his decision and give the baby a nickname: Mur. At the same time you rechristen Alya with her true name, Ariadna, now that she is older and will be a second mother to her little brother while you write.

Writing the same as breathing, as living.

The baby entrusted to his sister, you cover your pages with ink persuaded he will read them one day. Immersed in the blue of your baby's eyes, the blondness of his hair, you write snippets of lines then erase them right away. Words have left you. Your inspiration gone with the blood of the delivery. You are now just a woman like so many others. You are hopeless. Poor and hopeless.

With Sergei's grant at an end, you don't know whom to ask for money to pay the grocer, the butcher, the baker. You write to Pasternak the way one throws a stone in a well. His answer arrives in the form of a cheque. You run to the first bank and present it to the teller.

'But who are you, madame?' he asks, warily.

'A Russian emigre, sir.'

'Without an account, this check must be returned to the sender.'

The sound of a guillotine, the window coming down with a bang.

The horizon is dark, the literary journals are publishing less and less poetry. You can't do anything with your hands except write.

Back home, you write this in your notebook:

I could have been the foremost poet of my time. I know this because I have all the facts, all the talent but the times don't like me, and I don't like them, either. I don't recognize them as mine.

Writing isolates you from the emigre writers whom you consider 'pale relics of those who live on Soviet land'.

Except Marc Slonim who escapes your contempt.

You could have relied on him if he hadn't left you for someone else and if Bakhrakh, whom you never happen to see, occupied fewer of your thoughts.

You continue to write to him despite his silence. You defend yourself although he doesn't hold anything against you.

'I am incapable of hurting or inflicting pain on someone close,' you write to him . . . 'I cannot build my happiness on the bodies of others. I am not a conqueror and so I have decided to leave Rodzevich, who can live without me, whereas Sergei needs me.'

Without a man to love, you pour your love onto your baby. You walk him in a carriage during the day, you knit booties, hats, blankets by lamplight in the evening.

You want to be irreproachable, praiseworthy like Akhmatova who has given up writing or speaking out at all since the arrest of her son and the death of her husband executed by Stalin's police.

A recognized poet at 17 and the daughter of the great historian who created the Fine Arts Museum, you have been desired by many men. Your social life in Moscow was in full swing when the country began to crumble under your feet. None of the great minds you frequented could imagine what was going to happen: October 1917 was unimaginable.

Unimaginable the notion of living far from Moscow and being separated from the man you would marry.

You give the baby a breast with one hand and write to Bakhrakh with the other, he had become your obsession. You snub him or cajole him depending on your mood of the moment.

'You talk about friendship for me and love for another. Live with the other, live through others, marry them, but love me.'

Judicious advice dispensed by an experienced person who knows what she's talking about. Didn't you love Prince Wolkonsky, 60 years old and who didn't like women, that way?

You go from Wolkonsky to Rodzevich.

'Left at the apex of love. After ruining his life and mine. A serious motive: he wanted a simple life together, which none of the others who have loved me ever envisioned. We were doomed to be separated.'

A break-up told to Pasternak years later, then to your friend Olga who was always ready to listen to you, to excuse you and to pardon you when you spoke of Alya like a servant, Alya whom you pitied since she had no other distractions than the bucket, the mop, and gathering dead wood, forgetting your great connection during the years of destitution in a Moscow ravaged by war.

The precocious little girl who sat across from you, at the same table, writing a journal complementing yours, transformed into a housemaid.

Alya wrote of hunger, cold, fear, but also of the crowd of men surrounding her mother.

Your daughter could have been a great scholar if you had not relegated her to domestic chores under the pretext that you had to write. That you had a destiny.

With her father gone for three years, not knowing if he was still alive, the little eight-year-old girl found the nocturnal visits of your lovers at the time completely normal; all means to survive were acceptable. Nothing was reprehensible; the terrible death of Irina, the trials endured since you were banished from your family house, excused your excesses.

Back in Moscow in the midst of the civil war, you found the house empty. The furniture stolen, a casket sitting in the middle of the drawing room. In the casket, the last occupant of the place, the head of police who had hanged himself for reasons that were never made clear.

Embellishing the scene entirely, describing it to the child as if it were a good joke. You laughed. Alya clenched her teeth so not to burst into tears.

Her mother's life, a tragicomedy.

Alya understood better than anyone your excesses, your lovers, especially the last ones. You needed to be protected, her father was incapable of protecting you.

With a face as smooth as a stone, Sergei seems younger than you. An eternal adolescent, eternal student, he goes every morning to the university, his book bag in hand. Seen as a serious student by his professors, he comes home at night and does his homework at the table where you write to your lovers.

You refuse to take pity on him, your misery is greater than his.

Can your need to be protected be explained by the early loss of your mother?

You throw yourself headlong onto people, drown them under the waves of your feelings, demand that they listen. They must share your unhappiness, accept your justifications. Declare you innocent.

The death of little Irina whom you could have saved if you had taken her out of the orphanage at the same time as Alya, that death hidden for years rises up in your consciousness ever since the birth of Mur.

You talk about it for the first time with Sergei although you forbade him from doing so in order not to open what you called your wound.

You tell the father about the starving little girl, turning around you like a puppy around its master, begging for a crust of bread, a bit of milk, with the only word she was able to say: 'coo, coo' until she died from exhaustion repeating the same refrain, and her burial in the same pink dress she had worn for three months, so dirty and stiff it looked like it was made of the same cardboard as her coffin.

These facts that you have had time to digest have a different effect on him.

You don't expect such distress. Sergei sobs like a barking dog. He grieves both for Irina and for his inability to protect his family, to earn a living for them; without his student grant, living in Prague becomes untenable.

Why not move to France since Olga Chernova has invited you to share her three-room apartment on rue Rouvet in the 19th arrondissement, not far from the canal Saint-Martin?

The map of France spread out on the table, you stick pins on the places you will visit, certain you will go.

1. The Victor Hugo house on 6 place des Vosges.

2. Proust's house on boulevard Malesherbes and the Grand Hôtel de Cabourg.

3. The Anna de Noailles house, 22 boulevard de la Tour-Maubourg.

4. The Edmond Rostand house, 14 rue Monteaux in Marseille.

5. Place de l'Ile-de-La-Réunion where André Chénier was beheaded.

6. Your last visit reserved for Van Gogh, your brother in suffering, at the cemetery of Auvers-sur-Oise.

Used to the life of a nomad, here you are again sorting through your belongings deciding what you should take and what you should leave. Pieces of junk, old bohemian dresses. Worn-out furniture, worn linen, mismatched, chipped dishes. Mustn't be burdened.

You hesitate to take the baby buggy given by the team at the *Russian Gazette* including Marc Slonim who left you for another, but who takes care of the formalities so you can enter France.

So, no buggy. You'll rely on your arms, your legs . . . You want to know what the rue Rouvet looks like, if there is a park nearby, if the neighbours are noisy. Decline, in that case; you write to your prospective hostess:

> Mur the future musician sleeps lightly. He'll be a soldier, too, unless he joins the revolution, goes to prison, then I'll bring him packages.

Olga Chernova reassures you about the neighbours and you obtain authorization to go to France, so you leave Prague with a light heart. You never liked that city nor its inhabitants. The thought of spending another winter in Všenory horrifies you.

Through the train window you show Mur the country you are leaving and promise he'll live like a king in the one that awaits you.

The magic of breathing, your breath creates a four-leaf clover on the window. A good omen for what is coming next. You once again have faith in life.

Goodbye Prague, goodbye expat writers and artists who bad-mouthed you, disapproved of your behaviour. They were less vicious toward you in Moscow during the dark years, sharing the same misery made them more tolerant.

You can see them again, starving, skinny, taciturn.

Bernstein rolled his tobacco in newspaper, Andrei Biely sought out his adoptive father to squeeze a few rubles from him, then drank until he rolled on the ground and slept there through the night, Zamyatin attached the soles of his shoes with string, Mandelstam and his wife lived off begging, Akhmatova's small pension paid for the cigarettes she needed to cope since she no longer wrote and the name of her son had appeared on the list of future deportees.

Only Maxim Gorky who was a refugee in Switzerland lived comfortably, he opened his home to all who arrived from Russia: ambassadors, commissioner of the people, or a sailor in the Soviet navy could be found at his home.

He entertained everyone despite the exasperation of his lover Maria Fyodorovna; her harsh opinions of her countrymen were never changed by the guests who were interested only in the contents of their plates. What did it matter if their host detested Dostoyevsky, despised Gogol, ridiculed Turgenev, what they ate was of the highest quality thanks to the chef who stole from his employer.

Gorky's table, their revenge on the years of hardship when kasha and potato peels were all they ate.

'Better fed now thanks to help from the West, Russian emigres have lost their humanity,' you shout at the top of your lungs.

Forced to spend time with them during your three-week stay in Berlin you forgot them as soon as you arrived in Prague.

No reason to hobnob with them again after Pasternak went back to Russia; the Iron Curtain having closed on him, you made do with the company of Marc Slonim before someone else replaced you in his heart.

No regrets. Always ready to relive the same break-ups and the same infatuations with others. Your hand striking the air behind your shoulder banished the good and bad memories.

Paris with its Russian cultural centre, its Russian journals and newspapers, is waiting for you. The French you learned as a child will make the transition easier. You've translated a good number of Russian and German poets into French. Among others Rilke who told his friend Pasternak to thank you personally. You saw for the first time the man who knocked on your door. You hadn't read anything of his at the time. You couldn't have imagined the important place he would occupy in your life. The only one who responded to your call the day before your suicide.

Paris, 1925

Where have you wandered off to this time, Marina?

All morning long you've been looking at the same street, the same Metro station and the people it swallows up. You couldn't have imagined that Paris would be so sad. The rain that hasn't stopped falling since you arrived is fraying your nerves. You follow its flow on the window pane to drown out the bedlam around you.

You want to mute the fighting of Olga's children, Mur's crying as he lies squeezed into his basket. No room for a crib in 12 square meters.

Eight people crammed into two bedrooms. You can't write or read even a page of the book open on your lap.

Go far away, you keep repeating to yourself, move to the other side of the world, to a land of sun with people who don't run but walk, greet each other, stop to exchange news, smile. You dislike the French with their worried faces, their haste to go home after work, their lack of friendliness. No one greets you, no one looks at your baby. No one knows who you are.

In the evening, you don't turn around so you won't see the one who is coming up behind you. Sergei is carrying your distress on his narrow shoulders. He knows you're disappointed but has no solution to help. You close your eyes when he talks to you, squeeze your eyelids shut. You've decided not to gift him your tears.

'The man who bears on his shoulders a basket of tears,' you would write if you had a table to write on.

Three beds, a basket, and a chest of drawers, that's all you have left after 30 years of life. Left on a Moscow sidewalk, your books have certainly been burned in a fireplace; gnawing hunger removes any desire to read. Your furniture left in Prague, your dresses recycled into rags. Poorer than Job, more destitute than the beggar woman who futilely holds out her hand to passers-by rushing home, you don't know what to do with your existence, unliveable under any sky, ugly in all directions.

A stranger where you now are. Incapable of identifying yourself to your compatriots born out of the revolution, nor to the exiled recycled into taxi drivers, bartenders, labourers, cooks, or 'models' to avoid saying prostitutes when they are women.

You're not a White Russian, either, much less a Bolshevik. Invited to tea at the home of one of your countrywomen, a rich bourgeoise intrigued by your renown, you find yourself among women decked out in old-fashioned dresses but with magnificent jewellery.

You were to tell them about Moscow fallen prey to civil war.

Compassion or curiosity, the questions asked between two sips of a warm beverage leave you perplexed.

'Is it true you ate rats?'

'Did the Mandelstams in their exile eat chickpeas at every meal?'

'Is it true that Lilya Brik has changed lovers every week since her husband's suicide?'

'That dear Mayakovsky, to die so young, and from a bullet right in the heart.'

'All deaths are equal.'

The final word comes from the mistress of the house.

Frivolous, stuffy, falsely empathetic, you know you'll never see them again.

You decide not to answer any more of their questions, and stare at the paintings on the walls. You recognize the contemporary painters and cite their names like a child reciting her lesson: Khlebnikov, Kamensky, Malevich, Tatlin, Goncharova, and Wassily Kandinsky, the only one with both first and last names.

You stand up to get a closer look.

Seeing you riveted in front of a canvas, your hostess feels obliged to explain that she and her husband bought it half-heartedly.

'To encourage the artist,' she specifies.

You leave without saying goodbye to the rest of the guests.

You are a foreigner among your countrymen. A stranger everywhere, except in front of your notebooks.

A mistake coming to France. Knowing French doesn't guarantee you a roof, nor a job, much less friends. The French poets whom you translated into Russian, to absent followers. Whom you translated as if to take over their lives and forget your own.

A blunder, your reading of Mayakovsky's poems at the Russian cultural circle. The champion of communism, close to power, is unpopular with the bourgeois and aristocrats who came to listen to you.

Every day brings another disappointment.

The director of the *Nouvelle Revue Française* doesn't want your poems. His argument: 'They are neither Mallarméian nor surrealist.'

Nor do the other journals, including *Mercure de France*.

You're at a dead end. The darkness that falls at four in the afternoon draws in the four walls around you. They seem to be moving, pressing inwards to expel you.

You shouldn't have listened to Olga Chernova. The Paris of the tourist brochures and of poets is not the one that unfolds before your eyes. Buildings black with soot, the canal Saint-Martin where you walk with your son, filthy. Its water grim, beckoning suicide.

You walk for hours to avoid the cacophony of Olga's children, Alya's reproachful looks, Sergei's pained face. Too soft for you, that man who can't support you nor scratch your flesh with your nightgown.

You walk on the edge of the canal and of autumn, your eyes raised to the naked tree branches with a desire to give back to the trees the leaves destined to die under the feet of the passers-by.

The Ratcatcher (poem-tale) surges out of the black water of the canal. You write under the dictation of a flute-playing cat that attracts rats with its melodious tunes.

Writing, your only happiness.

You refuse to spend any more time in this neighbourhood. You need to breathe air, not the putrid air of the canal, to live within walls other than those on rue Rouvet. Out of the question, venturing into other arrondissements, you don't know how to take the Metro or the bus, hate Paris, whereas Sergei has fallen under its charm. He has visited all the monuments, spent an entire day at the Louvre. He walks from morning to evening, meets up with old friends with whom he concocts phantasmagorical plans. The former officer in the White Army is slowly turning Red, collaborating with Soviet agents in Paris; their mission: convince the exiles to return to their country though a large number of those who had returned were arrested as soon as they arrived. Considered traitors to the fatherland, they were sentenced, deported, sometimes executed.

The more Sergei gets involved, the more you become amorphous. As lazy as a garter snake; the glass of tea forgotten on the table would remain in the same spot for two days.

Yesterday, faced with the mountain of laundry to be washed in cold water, the water heater having broken, you made a wish. May the storm that was raging outside break down the door and carry you all away, may no one be left to tell what happened.

The Russian intellectuals whom you fled approach you. They like you, admire you, open the pages of their journals to you, invite you into their attic rooms with the same gestures of hospitality as in the past.

They live in isolation, speak Russian, eat Russian, goulash instead of steak, a samovar enthroned under each roof. Once the table is cleared, they dance to the sound of the balalaika, in a circle, a handkerchief waving in the air and their feet stomping on the ground.

You admire their spirit, share the 'parties' of these living dead who have turned their backs on the French society that doesn't want them.

Invited by one of your compatriots, a professor at King's College, for a two-week stay in London to read your poetry, you regain your taste for life and decide to leave rue Rouvet.

You choose a little town near les Sables-d'Olonne. La Vendée, land of the Chouans, suits your rebellious nature.

You desire the open sea, the horizon upon which to hang side by side your laundry and your dreams. Sergei who never says anything follows you without argument, but finds your decision to invite Olga and her three daughters incomprehensible when close quarters made writing impossible.

Stretched out on the beach, you read and write as long as there is daylight, write to Pasternak and especially Rilke.

Morose letters to the former who doubts his vocation as a poet whereas you doubt your vocation as a wife and mother.

Ardent letters to the latter, who is uneasy while also flattered by so much passion:

'Rainer Maria, may I call you that? You are poetry personified . . . What I expect from you Rainer is everything and nothing, that you allow me at every moment of my life to cast my eyes on you as on a mountain that protects me, on a guardian angel of stone . . .'

'Rainer don't be angry with me, I want to sleep, fall asleep with you, nothing more.'

You ask him permission to nestle your head on his left shoulder, to put your arm around his right shoulder, to know how his heart beats in his sleep.

'Rainer, night is falling, a train is howling. Trains are wolves; wolves are Russia; it isn't a train that is howling but all of Russia that is howling for you.'

Did he misunderstand the message, is that why he doesn't respond?

You write to him as one shouts fire:

'Dear Rainer Maria do you still love me?'

His silence ruins the final days of your stay in the Vendée.

Back in Paris you learn of his death in a sanatorium in Switzerland.

You learn the sad news from Marc Slonim who left you for another. He is soon coming to Paris and promises to visit you in the apartment that you share with four other emigre families, not far from Meudon.

Your throat is swelling with tears. You are consoled by telling yourself that Rilke belongs to you more dead than alive. He will henceforth live in you, you will share him with no one. Rilke will hold your hand while you write, blend his breath with yours. The same evening, you proclaim your certainty to your husband, accustomed to your exaltations.

One less man in your life. Two, he would say if he dared. He keeps to himself the news that would break your heart.

On January 13, the Russian New Year, you learn of the wedding of Konstantin Rodzevich and the young Maria Bulgakova, the daughter of the theologian Sergei Bulgakov in the orthodox cathedral on rue Daru.

'He doesn't have the right . . . ,' that's all you manage to say. The men who stop loving you are condemned to celibacy for life.

Your letter to your beloved ending your relationship is on your lips.

It had been raining for three days. An unseasonable, angry rain slapping the windows. Reflections of its drops on your page. The sky was mourning your separation. The impossibility of keeping your lover as well as your husband tortured you. Your tears added rain to the rain.

Back home you told your journal about your last embrace in a sordid hotel in Prague then drew a red line to separate what you were from what you would never be again.

You feel betrayed. No one loves you. Your correspondence with Pasternak cannot compensate for your debasing life as a housewife. Housework, shopping to buy what is least expensive at the market, the mountain of laundry to wash, the water that freezes in the bucket.

Your distress pushes you to the closest church, you light a candle, the flowing wax your diluted sorrow.

Your decline so rapid since you are no longer loved, love and success indissociable in you.

You are beginning to resemble the beggar woman in front of the orthodox cathedral on rue Daru, says Alya.

Difficult to recognize the Marina who once lit fires in the hearts of men in the woman who cooks and boils her laundry in the courtyard of a dilapidated building among women who have never read her books, any book.

The pack of Gitanes in the pocket of your housewife smock, the cigarette in the corner of your mouth burning itself down; your hands scrub, wring out, hang sheets, laundry, baby clothes on the same line.

The man approaching from afar waves his arms when he sees you. Marc Slonim surprises you.

Unlike you, your Prague lover hasn't changed. The hand you hold out to him is coarse, his is smooth; as smooth as his face.

You invite him to come in hoping he'll refuse. He promises to return another day—when you're not so busy.

'You'll have to wait until I'm dead, in that case.'

Slonim recognizes your determination to keep your head high, to make light of difficult situations.

You watch him walk away, then with a furious hand brush the ashes off your chest. You have decided to hurry death along, to put an end to your life by smoking more and more. To dissipate with the smoke, leave nothing to God with whom you are angry, nor to the devil who is not your friend.

The man who loved you entire afternoons in his attic room in Prague walks away without even a backward glance.

You laugh in order not to cry.

Your only weapons your sarcasm and new poems written with the blows of an axe, to destabilize, disconcert, upset.

Interjections and onomatopoeia follow each other like bullets from a machine gun. The expat journals refuse to publish them. One less source of income to pay your debts to the shops, to buy a coat for Mur and a tree for his first Christmas.

Lucid, your look at the woman in the mirror above the sink.

Wrinkled face and clothes so worn out, even the beggar in front of the orthodox cathedral on rue Daru wouldn't want them.

The package your sister Assia sent from London makes you laugh: two wool sweaters, socks, gloves, a pair of shoes. You laugh loudly, astonishing the speed at which you go from sadness to happiness, from despair to joy. Assia tells you that Gorky, who wants to meet you, is visiting.

A door is opening. You will run through it.

Gorky has friends in high places. He could intervene with the Kremlin to improve the lot of the Efron family, publish your work, give Sergei a job worthy of his abilities, perhaps enable a possible return to Russia; living in France has become hell.

Your sister promises you paradise, while you feel whole only in your notebooks, in front of a blank page. Is there a country in the world inhabited by people whose only occupation is writing? Writing until they can write no more without worrying about earning a living: a complete absence of money, authorities, formalities or any mail that didn't deal with the quality of a work or of writing.

You owe Gorky's imminent visit to Rilke who is watching over you from the other world. It is he who pushes the old writer who doesn't like your poetry to come see you. Rainer Maria is certainly reserving other surprises for you. Everything in its time. One must remain patient. The dead don't have the same sense of time as the living. Knowing he is protecting you gives you the strength to write. You feel his breath on your neck. He helps you choose words. You can trust him. The decision to return to Russia rests with him. Don't upset anything while Sergei is earning ten francs a day as an extra in a film about Joan of Arc.

As long as he pursues his Eurasian project and Mur is growing every day.

Satisfied with what he calls his work, Sergei doesn't seem in a hurry to go back to Russia, even if he has turned Red after having been White, even if the Bolsheviks are providing a little financing for his journal *Eurasia*.

Anyway, you see him so rarely. He only comes home to eat and sleep.

Sergei's phantasmagorical ideas raise him up above the fray. The wretchedness of his wife and children doesn't bother him. Knowing that you're living off the charity of compatriots as poor as you doesn't upset him, nor does the fact that his wife has had lovers. Always ready to share. Imperturbable, he doesn't worry when you don't have enough money for a baguette.

'There are people worse off than we are,' became his refrain.

Knowing that others are poorer than you raises him up in his esteem. The Khodasevichs have only a bed frame without a mattress, a samovar, two forks and a broom, the painter Lanskoy spends his days on the terrace of the Café de la Rotonde in front of a cup of coffee, Nina Berberova strings pearls, ten centimes a day, to feed her big sick man who leaves his bed only to visit the journal that has stopped publishing his articles. Khodasevich, the last witness to a prestigious era. He knew Chekhov, Tolstoy, Blok, shook Scriabin's hand.

Humiliated by his abrupt descent into poverty, he wants to die. Nina Berberova won't leave him alone for more than an hour. He might turn on the gas or throw himself out the window.

When you run into her on the street, you ask her if she is still writing.

'To write you have to have thoughts . . . '

Her response strikes you like a whip.

News from Russia reaches you with weeks of delay: Mandelstam's death in the Vladivostok camp breaks your heart. Died mad while reciting his poems under his moth-eaten blanket, hearing the mocking laughter of the other detainees as standing ovations.

Felt deep in your flesh, this death slides over Sergei.

Indifferent to everything, even to himself.

You no longer criticize him, he no longer looks at you. Ignored, the wife with the cigarette hanging from her mouth and the coffee cup in her hand. Coffee and cigarettes: your only pleasures after labouring all day long. In the evening you're done in, you sleep like the dead, dreamless sleep.

The only window in your life, your correspondence with Boris Pasternak who broke his promise to meet you in London for your readings at King's College but promises to attend the conference against fascism organized by the Soviets in Paris.

Aragon, Gide, Jouhandeau are among the honoured guests.

His absence in London mentioned in your letter in which you explained to him that it was the woman not the poet who had hoped to see him in that city.

> Understand me, Boris, I don't live to write but write to live. I don't write because I know but so I can know . . . The word is the path to the thing, not the opposite. (If it were the reverse one would need the word not the thing.)
>
> I need you like an abyss, the infinite to throw into and not hear the bottom.
>
> Love you, of course; I will love you more than anyone else but in my way, I completely I in the other . . .

You eagerly await the conference that will bring you together in Paris, the sun is working with you, the days go by more quickly.

Invited to the home of the poet Charles Vildrac, you encounter the writer Pilnyak, a friend of Pasternak's, and ask about his health.

' Perfect.'

'Thank God.'

'Right now he's staying with me in Lamskaia.'

'Was he evicted from his apartment?'

'No, he separated from his wife Evgeniya.'

'And their son?'

'He's living with his mother since Boris will be moving in with Zinaida Nikolaevna.'

A storm is rumbling in your head, the catastrophe of an encounter endlessly postponed has just occurred in this moment, on this chair. Suddenly everything is dark even though the weather is beautiful today.

Boris in Paris treats you like an old friend. You go with him to stores so he can buy presents for his young wife whose praises he sings:

'A perfect mistress of the house, an unparalleled decorator and cook.'

Then silence. You wish you were deaf so you won't hear any more but he insists on delivering the final blow.

'She's pregnant.'

He describes her to you, describes the rugs, the paintings on the walls, their spacious apartment in the Peredelkino residence made available to them by the Writers' Union.

No reason to fall apart, you blame no one, not even God. You have only to close your heart. One enters open doors without knocking, one leaves without thanking.

You want to be irreproachable, invite him to your home in Meudon where you have neither rugs, nor curtains, nor refrigerator.

Pasternak finds your miserable two-room apartment charming. Sergei, who takes him around Paris, charming. Mur and Alya who want to return and live in Russia, charming.

He can't understand your hesitation.

Misunderstanding across the board: he says he's given up poetry, given up lyricism which he considers an illness, defends the kolkhozes and service to the public cause.

The sound of glass breaking, his words in your ears.

You are disappointed in the poet, disappointed in the man. Useless to talk to him about your financial difficulties and your struggle to live, he quotes the philosopher Shestov who refuses to accept that this world that crushes us is the real one, supernatural enchantment.

You tell him you are suffering from no longer being published, he says that never being published didn't prevent Socrates from being Socrates.

You tell him your life is a desert since you are no longer loved. He says his own was like that before he met Zinaida.

Deaf to your cries of pain, the man whom you venerated for two decades.

Your confidences make him uncomfortable. He avoids your gaze, stares at the ground under his feet. You pull your skirt lower to hide your worn shoes.

Filled with happiness, Pasternak no longer has room for empathy. Indifferent to the misfortunes of others. A bitter fact: the passionate letters exchanged for years no longer have meaning for him. Zinaida has erased the past.

Pasternak goes back to his hotel, you sleep on the cold tile floor, your dress rolled up in a ball under your head.

Sleeping on a hard surface recommended for back pain though your pain is of the soul.

Your life is truly shattered ruins. You think about suicide without knowing how you would do it. Die like leaving, without leaving a body behind you.

But who would take Mur and Alya?

Useless to count on Sergei busy sticking up propaganda posters for his journal that no one buys.

You think seriously about ending your life and in your head write the note you would leave on the table.

Mailed before he left, Pasternak's letter thanking you for the 'friendly' visit doesn't reconcile you with life.

You answer with a bittersweet letter that he doesn't acknowledge.

Now at the hour of conclusions, my so-called harshness
was only . . . my defence against your sweetness, Boris.
Because at the last minute you let go of my hand to leave
me, stricken from the family of humans . . .

Dull and tasteless a life without Pasternak and without writing.

Useless to seek consolation among your compatriots.

They share neither your ideas nor the way you live.

During a meeting among exiles, you were so virulent Mur pulled your hand to leave. You sow hostility around you, like a bitter farmer throwing seeds into furrows.

The lines written in your notebook drip with despair.

'I am useless in France and impossible in Russia.'

You don't even want love any more: 'What should I expect with my face and my ash-coloured hair . . . '

Writing those lines, you don't know how much time you have left to live, nor if you will one day return to Russia. You know one thing: you are the most miserable being on Earth.

Writing and cigarettes kept your head above water. Now you don't write anymore and have no money to buy cigarettes. You fall back on butts kept for the worst days. You have a box full.

Your plight escapes no one. Pilnyak, whom you ask for 10 francs, gives you a 100, walks you home, and whispers news of Pasternak.

'Too much in love, too jealous, Boris made me swear never to look at his new wife.'

Short-lived sadness, Pilnyak's 100 francs will pay for the coal necessary to heat the apartment and for medicine for Sergei's cough which has kept him in bed for two weeks. You share with the walls the word tuberculosis whispered by the doctor but tell Alya and Mur to keep their distance when he coughs, to not drink from his glass, nor use his blankets, you alone are permitted to approach him.

Sergei ill and Pasternak torn from your reveries, you are like a wounded animal desperate to lash out.

You unleash your unhappiness onto people, objects, places:

'Paris gets a bit uglier every day. Its streets are straight out of a *roman noir* with their beggars on every corner.'

'The orthodox cathedral will one day crumble and fall into dust.'

Onto yourself, too: you see the same dust on your furniture and on your face.

'The expat poets aren't half as good as those who remained in Russia,' you write to Gorky who is vacationing in Sorrento, but you contradict yourself in another letter the next day.

'I prefer to spill my blood for literature than for a Russia abandoned by her true poets.'

A rudderless boat, any land you see seems good to land on.

Your friends avoid you. You smell like sulphur. The rain that streams down your windows is your only interlocutor. It hasn't stopped falling since Pasternak's departure. Its endless pounding suits the violence of your feelings. It comes in through the chimney, the holes in the roof. The cracks in the walls. Basins are overflowing. A rag in one hand, a bucket in the other, you sponge it up, wring the rag until your hands come off your arms. Deformed by arthritis, they have trouble writing.

'To be buried in the rain,' you note in your notebook, your only friend.

To die drowned or hanged is all the same to you who love the death of love and would have done it if Mur could survive alone.

A suicide waiting for the right moment to carry out the act, that's what you are.

Nina Berberova in her book *The Italics Are Mine* describes you alone talking to no one during the mass in memory of Prince Wolkonsky on rue Daru.

You wanted to be alone to stand apart from the others and prove to them that they weren't necessary in your life. Your two visits, one to your childhood friend Gala the wife of Éluard, the other to Elsa Triolet, followed by no others. You preferred to converse with your worktable, its worn wood and your face lined with the same fissures, the same wrinkles.

You sentenced yourself to solitude by not trying to dissuade Alya who complained of the amount of housework she did from leaving.

Your daughter held it against you for having interrupted her drawing studies at Goncharova's studio to take care of her brother and knit sweaters that she sold at markets to contribute to the household coffers.

Gone with her bundle of clothes on her shoulder, your Alya, after a fight that shook the walls.

Your companion of the dark years became closer to her father. They both want to go back to Russia whereas your Russia is not on the geographical map but on the sheets of paper you cover with your feverish writing, carried away with you in all your moves with the icon and the samovar, the only possessions you have left.

The same disillusionment from Moscow to Berlin, from Prague to Mokropsy, from Všenory to Paris, from Bellevue to Meudon, from Clamart to Vanves; the apartment in Clamart became too sad after Alya's departure then after Sergei's for Russia.

They left three months apart: Alya of her own free will, Sergei forced to flee, suspected of complicity in the assassination of a former KGB agent. Exfiltrated one night by the Soviet embassy; two inspectors from the French police soon burst into your apartment. They turned it upside down, searched your things, scattered the pages of your journal, seized all your papers, then took you to the police station escorted between the two policemen.

Interrogated for hours at the national security offices, your statements never varied. Sergei Efron is an intellectual, not a spy at all, he is a journalist and appears in films.

Sublime your defence of the fragile man wed when you were 19, he only 18, who never played the role of husband. Fighting with the Whites, student of philology in Prague, founder of a new concept—Eurasia—your Seryozha is an idealist, absolutely not an assassin.

You interspersed the great deeds of your hero with the rantings of Corneille, Racine, and your own verses.

They were stunned.

Persuaded they were dealing with a mad woman, they let you go late that night.

'They didn't beat me, at least there's that,' you told Mur who was worried while you were gone.

He saw you arriving in the darkness, bent over almost to the ground.

You looked like a beast of burden. The stairs climbed painfully, you threw yourself on the bed and fell into a sleep as deep as a well.

You kept to yourself the tense interrogation, the iron handcuffs around your arms as if to break your bones and prevent you from fleeing.

'It was routine,' you would tell him the next day, 'formalities regarding our situation. Normal for foreigners.'

Foreigners, Mur's ears accustomed to that word.

His friends make fun of his foreign accent, of his bizarre jackets sewed by his mother, of his wrinkled trousers.

'Doesn't your mother know how to iron?'

'My mother writes. She's the greatest poet in the world.'

He's the one who feeds you the next day, who heats up the soup of carrots, celery, peas, no potatoes, his mother ate them at every meal during the dark years in Moscow.

A consolation for you, the pack of cigarettes stolen behind the back of the shopkeeper who notices and calls the police. Taken to the station, interrogated, slapped, Mur is let go given his young age.

Between two bouts of sobbing he promises not to do it again, not to steal again and to bring home better grades to the one who keeps telling him:

'Study, Mur, to become a groundskeeper, so you won't be a grave-digger.'

You love madly this boy born of three fathers.

You tolerate all his pranks: the lifeline in the hollow of his hand is as short as yours. You and Mur will not have long lives. A seducer, he knows how to soften you up with little gifts (not calling them thefts); the package of real coffee placed on the stove yesterday made you swallow your scolding.

He returns home at night later and later. Does he have friends? With whom does he spend time? You sleep badly, watch his comings and goings through your sleep. The noise in the kitchen pulls you out of a dream: you're in your childhood house. A burglar is moving around the bottom floor. You can't get up to chase him away. His shape is not unknown to you. The stiff body, the hair combed back are those of Mandelstam. He is wearing the same grey striped suit he wore 20 years ago when he had joined you in Moscow and you had rejected him. You know he is dead but you're not surprised at his presence in your house at this hour of the night. You know he is dead but don't tell him so you won't sadden him. You also know that you're dreaming and that you only have to open your eyes to put an end to this situation.

He owes you an explanation and offers it without hesitation.

He learned that you have real coffee, arabica, and couldn't resist the temptation to come and taste it.

The cup raised to his lips, he slurps a mouthful, sighs with pleasure, swallows down the rest then asks you to give a message to his wife Nadezhda.

'But where can I find her? Your wife is hiding so she won't suffer your fate.'

'On the other side of the country,' he says slyly.

Seeing that you don't believe him, he takes a coin out of the pocket of his jacket, tosses it in the air then catches it on the back of his hand.

'I told you it was tails.'

Spinning around, he is already outside. Gone without thanks.

Awake, you think about Nadezhda who spends no more than three days in the same place, avoids cities, lives off the generosity of those who venerate the memory of her husband.

'There are people more wretched than I,' you tell yourself and try to go back to sleep.

Pasternak's face forces itself on you whenever you can't fall asleep.

A busy husband, attentive father, a member of the nomenklatura, his increasingly short responses to your letters leave no echo in your heart. You no longer have 'your seat in his life' as his first letter, two decades old, had proclaimed.

Pasternak has taken back the only gift he ever gave you: exaltation.

You blame your despair on everything around you.

The mirror above the sink is responsible for your wrinkles.

Too narrow, the worktable is guilty of drying up your inspiration.

Too noisy, your neighbours prevent you from concentrating.

They hole up at home, let the storm pass when you open your door and scream at them to stop their cacophony.

The madwoman on the third floor who writes will eventually calm down.

Only your neighbour on the same floor, Monsieur Koursk, a Trotskyist sought by Stalin's agents, knows who Marina Tsvetaeva is. He waits for your door to close to put a bowl of goulash and a glass of vodka on your doorstep.

Yesterday, he added your first collection of poems, with a request for a dedication. He must be looking through the peephole to have picked it up a minute later.

Monsieur Koursk didn't see the tear in the corner of your eye. Nor does he know that this collection published in Russia

15 years ago has disappeared from circulation. The poems by the wife of Sergei Efron who fought with the vanquished Whites, his name concealed from the authorities.

To my neighbour on my landing and in my heart.

Your friend, Marina Tsvetaeva,

You write to the man whose face you haven't seen, and whose real name you don't know (Koursk is a pseudonym), you know only his meatballs and his cat named Leon, sometimes Lenin.

Monsieur Koursk isn't familiar with the inside of your apartment reduced to three mattresses and a table, but with your shouts when you curse the inhabitants of the building who play dead while waiting for the storm to pass.

Your shouts absorbed by the walls of the stairway, you throw on your coat and walk to the train station, passing by the open market where the vegetable sellers keep their unsold items for you.

The same trek every evening. You never miss the arrival and departure of the train that goes to Le Havre and the boat that will one day take you back to Russia, far from a France that did not know how to appreciate you. That humiliated you.

Back home, that night after the police station, you stop short when you see the crowd outside the apartment building. The police are there for you. They're going to arrest you again. You would run away if an officer doesn't jostle you. He's not interested in you, but in the body that is lying on the ground in a pool of blood. A cat is pacing around it, meowing.

You recognize the man by his cat. Fallen from a window on the third floor, he died instantly.

There's talk of suicide, of assassination, but under one's breath.

Someone has learned through someone else who in turn heard it from someone else that Koursk was hiding under a false identity and that two individuals were watching his comings and goings.

'He did his shopping in the evening, when they were gone.'

'Didn't see anyone. Didn't speak to anyone.'

You wanted to speak up, talk about his goulash and your poems that he read, but no sound comes out of your mouth. The dead are as heavy as lead.

You imagined him an old man, but you discover someone who is barely 30.

The rigid body on the stretcher inserted into the doors of the ambulance, the gapers scatter. The pool of blood, you and the cat are the last ones to leave.

You would stay there if it wasn't for Mur's voice calling you from the window. He witnessed the scene and saw his mother freeze, as if turned into a statue.

The cat climbs the stairs behind you, follows you inside after a pause in front of its owner's apartment which now cannot be entered due to official tape and a wax seal on the door.

A cat at home?

Your son is both delighted and worried.

'Cats don't eat soup,' he points out.

' . . . but mice. Which aren't lacking in the building.'

A cat to share your melancholy and your sadness.

It lost its owner, you lost the man you loved.

In love with another, Pasternak is dead to you.

His virtual death soon followed by the real ones of Andrei Biely, Voloshin, and the poet Nikolay Gronsky under the wheels of a metro train at the Pasteur station.

'I was his first love, he was my last,' you note in your note-book. The young literary critic, 18 years old, took you on long walks in nature, as far as Versailles or elsewhere. Wouldn't have left you if he hadn't fallen in love with a young woman his age who quickly abandoned him.

He knocked at your door one night and you didn't open it. It was raining hard. The same storm raged in the sky and in your chest. You told him to go back to his parents' house:

'I am old and worn out. I no longer have a body or hands for love.'

Unlike Ehrenburg, Pasternak, Biely, Voloshin, and Slonim, Gronsky who died young did not leave a body of work behind him.

Alya who knew him well must mourn him if she can still cry, you bitterly say to yourself.

You have news of her through the grapevine. She's living with a certain Samuel Mulia, a middle-aged married man with children. She is working in a museum, but doesn't have time to write to her mother.

The French journals that rejected your poetry seem to like your prose. Your biographical pieces on Gorky, Blok, Pasternak, Akhmatova, Biely, Mayakovsky, and Voloshin open doors for you.

Invited to a party in the home of Natalie Clifford Barney, you encounter Gide, Henri de Régnier, Aragon, Marcel Jouhandeau, Renée Vivien, Lise Delharmes, Marie Bashkirtseff, a young woman of 24 who doesn't hide her taste for women, nor her distaste for motherhood:

'Any laundress can have children.'

Your relationship with Natalie Barney goes back to 1920. You wrote to her after the reading of Remy de Gourmont's *Letters to the Amazon*.

'We will be more than wives, sisters, mothers. We will be female brothers as a man,' she had replied.

'You, my female brother, you are closer to me, like every unique person, especially like every unique female person' you had written to her by return mail.

And now here you are in her home on rue Jacob among her illustrious guests.

You are surrounded, embraced, listened to. No one contradicts you when you criticize the Nobel committee for having chosen Bunin over Gorky. They applaud the originality of your faded skirt, your beret drawn down to your ears, your gypsy earrings and your sandals in the middle of winter.

They insist on seeing you again but don't call you back. You will never be part of their world, you know it and write it to your friend the actress Anastasia Tukalevskaia:

> The French have good manners. In 14 years no one has
> laughed in my face. I've defied Paris, its fashions, its taste,
> in a thousand ways: by the lack of makeup on my face,
> my grey hair . . . and my big shoes.

From the party at Natalie Barney's you retain the memory of beautiful women in beautiful dresses, moving around in a beautiful setting. Bowties and tails required, difficult to distinguish the guests from the waiters, or the wives from the mistresses, the men who like women from those who prefer men.

Falsely affectionate, frivolous, flatterers; the impression of attending a performance, the curtain falls, one leaves the place.

You don't recall a thing about what you've just seen.

Back to Vanves on the last train, you become a housewife like all other housewives again.

A broom in one hand, a pen in the other in case an idea arises, you watch for the mailman who announces your letters from Russia by honking three times. Running down the stairs you give him the foreign stamps for his collection and hug the envelopes to your breast.

Alya, Sergei tell you about their life in the communal apartment they share with four other families.

Your sister Assia tells you about her work in Gorky's office when he returned to Russia.

Occupied with his young wife and their move into the Peredelkino residence reserved for friends of the regime, Pasternak doesn't write to you anymore whereas letters given to trustworthy people or by way of the diplomatic pouch arrive in three days.

You wonder how lovers corresponded in Antiquity. No mailmen in those days, nor mail boxes opened with a clinched heart, but clay tablets engraved by scribes, baked, then carried on the back of a donkey, or a camel, from province to province, sometimes for months before reaching the recipient.

Time having passed, you are surprised that Pasternak hasn't responded to your bitter letter written the day after his departure.

Dead? You would have learned of it in the press. The doubt that sinks into you makes an oily spot, touches Vyacheslav, Lann, Parnok, Ehrenburg, Biely, Vichniak, Bakhrakh, Slonim, Rodzevich.

Why does everyone stop loving you?

Your question knocks around your head like a fly against a window.

They approach, they are afraid, they disappear . . .

My demands, I demand absolutely nothing.

The thing is that while I'm seeing them, they don't seem bored.

Total and complete disappearance, he gone I alone.

They leave me without a word, without a farewell. They came—they will no longer come. We wrote—we will no longer write. And here I am in the great silence that I never break, wounded to death . . . Without ever having understood anything . . . not how nor why.

You reserve your last embers of love for Salome Halpern who helps you hang on. Salome living at a distance, you write to her every day.

If I were with you at this moment, it is certain—I know myself—I would plunge into you, hide in you, sheltered from everything in you: from the day, the century, the world, your eyes and mine which are no less merciless; consciousness is sometimes non-knowing, misunderstanding, forgetting.

Salome thank you for that night richer, greater . . .

You are suffering from solitude, Salome is reluctant to be seen with you.

The emptiness around you since the departure of Alya and Sergei and the suicide of Nikolay Gronsky. You frighten your neighbours, the shopkeepers who don't dare ask you to pay your debts.

To reunite your family has become your obsession since Pasternak in a letter from months ago advised you not to return to Russia.

'Don't come back to Moscow, it's very cold here because of the air that escapes.'

A veiled message, but how can you fight against solitude? And should you wait for a miracle for those who consider you a good biographer to finally be interested in your poetry, for them to read your last collection *The Lad* written directly in French?

'I'm like the cuckoo, I hide my eggs in the nests of other birds.'

You hide your poetry under your prose so it will be read.

Hide your love for Pasternak under passing infatuations so not to suffer.

Pride displayed in every circumstance despite the hand you hold out in a gesture of begging.

So many paradoxes in such a small little woman.

As skinny as the cuckoo to which you allude: you shout loudly to impose your ideas and climb up on your high horse, sure that your head will ultimately touch the sky though inside you are grovelling.

You suffer from not being recognized for your poetry while you are for your prose.

'Here I am a poet without readers, in Russia I am a poet without books.'

Only the idea that you have a destiny prevents you from sinking. You're waiting for a miracle, the recognition of those who don't believe in you. You are stung by the rejection of your translation of Pushkin's poetry for the celebration at the Sorbonne of the centenary of his death.

'The organizer used the translations of a young girl, friend of some man,' you note bitterly in your journal.

You worked for 6 months, 200 poems adapted for the tastes of the time whereas the young woman friend of some man translated literally, respecting the order of the words. A heavy, incomprehensible result:

> You told me when we met
> Under an eternally blue sky
> In the shadow of the olives
> The kisses of lovers will reunite my friend again.

Instead of your 'not selected' words:

> You told me: tomorrow my angel
> Over there at the end of the horizon
> Under the orange tree laden with fruit
> Our hearts our lips will be joined
>
> For your land of beautiful fables
> For the laurel trees of your fatherland
> You abandoned that fatal land
> You left stripping me of life.

No room for a foreigner in the temple of literature. Your great talent as a poet and translator rejected by the Sorbonne and by the director of the *Nouvelle Revue Française*, publisher of the acts of the colloquium.

Useless to curse the times or throw stones at them. The times are not a dog. The times are not your friend.

A door slammed in your face, your translations are returned. You are relieved to obtain the two visas for Russia in your name and in Mur's.

The Bolsheviks pardon you after having condemned you.

You owe this reversal to your sister's intervention through Gorky who has friends in high places.

Assia has decided that your life is in Russia alongside your husband and daughter and not in that France which was unable to appreciate the great poet that you are.

For the seventh time in seventeen years, you sort through your things deciding what you should take and what you should abandon. Places without a soul. Empty, the seats around the table. The ashtray fills up as the house empties. Trembling, your hand that crushes the butt. Joints ravaged by arthritis. The words flee them. And why write? No publisher for Tsvetaeva in France, those in Russia have changed their profession, perhaps executed or dead from natural causes.

Boxes you collect from the shops filled to the brim with only that which is necessary in your life: your manuscripts and your books, you leave behind: linen, dishes, and kitchen utensils.

You hesitate to keep photo albums: there's no resemblance between the young woman with the hourglass figure and the hungry mouth and the old woman you have become. Through what strange mutation has the former engendered the latter?

The place tidy when you return the keys to your landlady. Only the impressions of your bare feet in the dust tell of your stay between the walls.

You don't know your neighbours, so no farewells to anyone.

Seventeen years of life abroad packed into a few boxes and a suitcase stuffed with manuscripts to which you add your heart.

Kneeling in front of the icon, you and Mur make the sign of the cross as you have done in every move.

You pray to God that the boat won't sink, that Pasternak, Sergei, and your sister Assia will meet you at the landing, that the Writers Union will publish your poems, and that your family will finally be reunited under the same roof.

You take advantage of the final moments to write to Anna Nikolaevna and Adriana Berg who helped you in difficult moments.

You thank them for the coat that helped you get through the winter, for the blue dress that helped you see through the darkness, for Mur's trousers which hugged his beautiful bum so closely, for the buttons, the shirts, the coffee, the books, and the visit to the old cemetery.

You thank the hands that raised you up when you were unable to rise.

'You are the last person to whom I'm writing,' you tell Adriana. 'The house is asleep, Mur is asleep. Just a good old woman who doesn't sleep. She is sitting on my skin. The good woman is me.'

Seventeen years tossed behind you, you go toward the unknown.

What awaits you when you arrive? Will Sergei find you aged?

Will Pasternak meet you?

And how can you reform the ties that bound you to Alya?

You decide not to argue with her anymore; your last fight, a wound that never healed. Alya the meek transformed into a furie. She flung into your face everything she had held back in 20 years of cohabitation. Your demonic egotism, the list of your lovers, your anger when she balked at doing your housework for you.

Her bundle of clothes on her shoulder, she continued in the stairwell to recite the list of your misdeeds. Six floors: 12 renters who laughed discreetly, delighted to see you besmirched by your own daughter.

They wouldn't have dared.

You frightened them. Frightened your friends.

'Arrogant, filled with self-importance, she overestimates herself,' they said behind your back.

You leave, your heart heavy with resentment towards a France that didn't recognize you, towards a Russia that exiles, executes its poets who don't bow down before those in power.

Mandelstam dead in the Vladivostok camp. Mayakovsky dead by his own hand from a bullet in his heart.

You can still hear the shot that went through his chest, continue to hear his final words: 'The boat of love has run aground on everyday life.'

Should his suicide be attributed to a fight with his wife Lilya Brik or to Stalin's disfavour?

How then to explain Lilya Brik's intervention with Stalin so that Mayakovsky's work would be recognized?

'Not to love Mayakovsky's poetry is a crime' Stalin, partially guilty of the poet's suicide, had said.

Lies, hypocrisy, mystery.

Too late to lose heart. You've decided to leave. Your destiny demands it. You do it for Mur who doesn't like France, doesn't like his school or his classmates. He is your only son, engendered by the three men you have loved.

Your tears held under your eyelids, you close the suitcase holding your manuscripts, sit on it, ready to return to Russia, ready to confront those who are cleaning up the country with rounds of massacres.

You are exhausted. A half-century running after love and words has done you in.

Poems, essays, translations, notebooks have accompanied you in all your moves. Never out of your sight your notebooks, your journal, the drafts of your poems and manuscripts whereas men were fleeting. Disappeared.

The boat arrives at the port, Mur looks out over the crowd and finds his sister.

Alya's arms wave wildly over the heads.

Is the bald and paunchy man with her the Samuel Mulia you were told about?

Hugs, tears, kisses. She tells you that your sister Assia has been deported and that an ill Sergei is waiting for you in Moscow, he's been living with his sister Elizaveta while waiting for lodging to be assigned.

'And where will we sleep?' Mur wonders.

'At Elizaveta's, too.'

'Why not with you?'

'Because I live with Samuel.'

Mur, disappointed, kicks at the ground.

No Sergei, no Pasternak on the quay.

Leningrad seems infinitely ugly to you.

So much effort and agitation to end up here.

Seventeen years away from your country, you find the same city but dustier and more barren. Public squares razed, replaced by utilitarian buildings. A city transformed into a propaganda poster. And no Pasternak to meet you. Did living in Peredelkino with the nomenklatura distract him from the date of your arrival of which you did, however, inform him?

Morose faces in the train to Moscow. No exchanges between travellers. Caution is advised, the NKVD which hears the slightest confidences classifies people into two categories: traitors or heroes, good citizens or enemies of the people.

Alya responds to your questions with short words. She doesn't have any news of your sister Assia exiled for two years in a republic of the Caucasus, her father very ill. Tuberculosis.

Seventeen years away from your country, you find Moscow colder, more barren. Fewer restaurants, squares, movie theatres, but more factories, youth centres, and administrative buildings.

Exhausted by the trip, you must still receive Elizaveta's neighbours and acquaintances who come by to present their wishes for a happy return to the great poet whom they know by name only.

Shoes left on the doorstep, hugs, affectionate taps on the shoulder, the forced happiness veers into gloom. They look at you and shake their heads with incomprehension. They want to know why you returned and if you have memories of the Moscow that you once knew.

You answer as few questions as possible, avoid asking about former friends, who perhaps fell into disfavour, don't press when they tell you that they don't know whether such and such a person is still alive.

They're in no hurry to go home. Home being comprised of communal apartments, they are just as happy in someone else's place.

Are they going to sleep here? You're worried.

Ghosts, those who have survived the war and hunger.

Their former world has departed with its language, no more lovely phrases, no citing of poets, but a vocabulary reduced to the useful: a card for supplies, a card to access the canteen, a membership card for such and such an organization.

They exchange survival tips, talk amongst themselves.

You don't have any of those cards. Nor does Sergei; never exonerated despite his activity helping to repatriate Russian emigres wanting to return home.

Suffocated by coughing fits your husband is more suspect than ill. Stalin has deported many of his former collaborators; his trembling due as much to fear as to fever.

The intimacy you dreamt of postponed until you move into your own apartment, Alya promises you.

In close contact with the NKVD, her Mulia is working to obtain a place where you can stay.

The seven people inhabiting the apartment are joined by five others, former friends: poets, literary critics, painters.

They want to see Marina lost from sight ever since a wall has separated the USSR from the rest of the world.

The fear of being arrested, deported, shot at any moment has erased everything from their memories. They remember a little about you. Lann remembers your glasses and the square cut of your hair. Vyacheslav has vague memories of your affair, though he describes in minute detail the shambles in which you lived. Voloshin dead a year earlier is missing from the group.

He's the one you most hoped to see, he who had written the first article on your poems, had given it to you in your grandparents' house in Tarusa where you were spending the summer. You were 17, he was twice that.

You have retreated in their memories. Hunger the only survivor of the dark years, they tell you every detail of it as if you hadn't lived through it.

Your friends invited to share your meagre meal, Lann inhales in one gulp his bowl of soup, his head leaning backward, taps on his belly, says he's content to see you again then heads to the door. Vyacheslav who loved you in the time when you no longer knew if you had a husband doesn't ask about Sergei in bed in the adjoining room, but about Alya 'who wrote such nice little poems inspired by those of her mama.'

Faces contract when one of them mentions Irina.

There's no room for the child who died from hunger between the plates wiped with a loaf of bread.

They avoid looking at each other, looking at you, all get up at once. They promise to return but don't know when.

The main thing: move around as little as possible so not to attract attention to yourself, to be less visible.

Mentioning Irina threw cold water on the group.

You're trembling even though it's warm outside. Moscow has never had such a hot summer. You feel under your feet the snow turned to ice when you left the orphanage leaving Irina to her fate. You struggled to walk with Alya in your arms. Fog and darkness suddenly obscured your sight.

You had trouble finding your way back to Moscow, would have died of cold with your daughter if not for the cart driver who stopped even though you no longer had a voice to hail him.

Forty days and nights to pull Alya from death, the same number of days and nights not asking about Irina. Collecting wood to make a fire, vegetables for soup, monitoring the temperature of the ill child occupied your days. And where could you find a telephone to call the orphanage?

Her mother gone with her sister, Irina left to herself.

Too small to reach her bowl of soup and her bit of bread, she died a few days later. Died from hunger in the orphanage where she was supposed to be fed.

Your friends stand up one after the other. They saw you drifting into your thoughts and did nothing to bring you back to them. Anyway, you are no longer the one they knew, perhaps loved.

Grey hair, grey eyes, grey dress, you look like a pile of ashes.

Contacted the next day, Pasternak agrees to meet in a subway station. You regain some hope and run to meet him. You recognize him in the distance in the crowd. Unlike you, he hasn't changed despite the wearing down of time and hearts. He has to go home in five minutes, Zinaida has invited friends to dinner. He constantly looks at his watch, is worried about Zinaida who doesn't tolerate tardiness, is worried about you helpless in the face of life. A concern of a lover even after the death of love. He shakes your hand like an old acquaintance, then walks away briskly.

The apartment promised by the NKVD is in Bolshevo, an hour from Moscow. It's where former agents are housed. Sergei Efron and Dimitri Klepinin worked together in Paris at the repatriation bureau.

Three rooms for three families, Alya and her Mulia who left his wife and children join you.

The household tasks shared among the three women, they assign you the dishes.

Constantly plunged in water, your hands peel, your nails fall off the skin. You scrape the bottom of pans, scrub, listen to your tears falling in the sink, empty the buckets of dirty water in the fields, far from the house to avoid the blood-sucking mosquitoes.

Your days in front of the sink, your nights torturing yourself. Unconscious from the medicine, Sergei sleeps. You would write if you were less exhausted and if the lamp lighted the page better. Restrictions on everything: gas, heating wood, sugar and flour. You and Alya invent unimaginable recipes to appease the hunger of Mur, transparently thin.

You no longer dream of glory, but of a table where you can write:

Don't knock on doors
Glory is a table corner
And an elbow leaning on it . . .
Faucets leak
Chairs scrape
Mouths speak full of gruel . . .

The only poem you wrote in those times.

It is during this daily hell that Alya is arrested. She thinks it's a misunderstanding and follows the two policemen offering small talk. She's sure she'll return that evening.

The days go by, you make the rounds of prisons and finally locate her in Lubyanka. She's accused of being the daughter of Sergei Efron whose activities in Paris weren't clear. The tortured girl ends up revealing what the father kept silent for years.

Twice a week you stand in front of the same window.

You tremble uncontrollably while the agent consults his papers. Scandalous the sound of your chattering teeth.

'Not on the list' means deported, maybe executed.

'On the list' makes you sob with gratitude.

And so, your package of sugar, tea and cocoa would be given to your daughter in Knyazhpogostsky. A district in the Komi Republic.

She writes to you to reassure you, to thank you for the package but doesn't say a word about the torture she's endured, nor about the haemorrhage due probably to a miscarriage.

Interrogated for three days and three nights by policemen who took turns, beaten, her body covered with bruises and wounds, she strongly denied her father's counter-revolutionary activities.

What did they squeeze out of her under torture to enable them to arrest Sergei in turn?

You spend your days running from one prison to the other with the fear you'll hear 'not on the list'.

On what are they basing their decision to sentence Alya to eight years of deportation?

The Klepinins in turn arrested and the lodging given to other agents, you and Mur are forced to leave.

Sergei's sister lets you stay temporarily in her two-room apartment in Golitsyno. You disappear when she gives her diction lessons, you and Mur spend your days outside waiting for night.

No room for your six cartons of books that left Paris three months ago and have just been delivered. Your sister-in-law can't stand clutter. Can't stand to be contradicted, either. Having stayed in Russia while others were hiding abroad gives her the right to impose her will under any circumstances.

Elizaveta spies on you whenever you move, forbids you from smoking, wipes off the seat as soon as you stand up. A maniac for order. Mur calls her Miss Stalin. You bless her for keeping you under her roof but curse her for rejecting your books.

You watch the eight cartons on the sidewalk like a mother hen her chicks. You pray to the heavens that it doesn't rain.

A cat you've never seen before is camped on them. Straight out of your work *The Ratcatcher* and from the black waters of the canal Saint-Martin, it protects your books from thieves. Did it come from Paris? Did it follow Mur who never got over the loss of Monsieur Koursk's cat?

With snow predicted for the coming days you're emboldened to ask for lodging from the Writers Union. You mention the services you rendered to Russian literature as a translator, not as a creator so as not to displease those who believe your work doesn't conform to the communist aesthetic.

The ten square meters for Mur, your books and you in a home for aging writers are welcome. Four blank walls, a light-bulb on the ceiling, but something unexpected: your meals at the canteen.

Translation work will pay for the heating and the rent.

You translate 25 lines a day, the rest of your time devoted to writing letters sent to anyone who might be able to look into the fates of your daughter and husband.

You write to Stalin, then to Beria a six-page letter to convince him of the innocence of Sergei Efron. Neither responds.

Pasternak doesn't dare intervene, Bukharin once so esteemed by Stalin could have been useful to you if he hadn't been arrested, sentenced, and executed.

Dead the same year as Mandelstam.

Stalin who had witnessed his trial through a window in the door of the tribunal had not intervened, but had nodded his head in a gesture of agreement with the death sentence.

Whom can one address if not God.

The churches you slip into while hiding in the shadows are devoid of God, the lit candles weep his death with large drops of wax.

You always finish your visits with a detour to the cemetery and are saddened when the two dates of birth and death are separated by so few years. So many interrupted lives.

In a village close to Voronezh only the cemetery is populated. The houses are empty. The roundups at the end of every day starting at six o'clock took away everything that circulated in the streets.

Mandelstam made himself as tiny as possible, hid while waiting for the end of the roundup; he breathed again when the bell of the town clock rang eight.

A pitiless time, it took only a hint, an anonymous letter, a false accusation to be arrested, deported, executed; those deported and shot smeared by their families so they wouldn't meet the same fate.

Sergei's case even simpler to explain. It was the custom for a new leader to eliminate the collaborators of his predecessor.

The Writers Union ultimately looked into your situation.

The place that awaits you in a retirement home is a gift from heaven. You are greeted with open arms before being rejected.

Your scathing opinions, your superior airs earn you the enmity of the other retirees. They snicker when you say you once knew Alexander Blok, Gorky, Bunin, Mayakovsky, or when you talk about your correspondence with Rilke and Pasternak.

Those who have read you criticize you for chopping up the language, breaking lines, being incomprehensible.

Persuaded that you are fabricating, they avoid you. Staying in your room, you binge on coffee, the coffee maker and you in a continual state of boiling over.

Your stay to be terminated at the end of the month, you are ordered to leave the premises. You pound the pavement all day long looking for any room not far from Moscow so Mur can continue going to school.

Back in your room in the evening without prospects, you look around for a place to hang yourself.

Undesirable everywhere, you would like to die but are hesitant to do it with your own hands. Rule out death by drowning or fire, you don't like either one. In fact, you'd like to disappear without leaving a body behind: no longer exist. Volatile.

Feeling a recurrence of friendship, Pasternak whom you call on for help intervenes with the director of the Writers House who assigns you a room in a communal apartment on 10 Herzen Street in Moscow.

The indignities begin as soon as you arrive: the current renters forbid you from drying your laundry next to theirs, take your kettle off the fire. You don't complain. A roof over your head to be able to write, that's all you ask.

Fear of a war with the Reich is stirring up passions.

Bags of sand around public monuments, blacked-out windows, the fear of bombings, create connections among you. You are no longer an emigre, much less a foreigner. You are finally accepted.

Sixteen years old, Mur who wants to join the army is assigned to civil defence.

The bombings get closer and closer to Moscow, the Writers Union suggests that its members retreat to the countryside. There are many of you climbing into the trucks that will transport you.

They are chatty, you have an absent look.

You neglect to get out at the first stop, in Chistopol, a true town. Too late to fix it. You are the only one to continue to Yelabuga.

Yelabuga, a farming village. Furrows extend to the horizon. No asphalt road, no stone houses, but izbas made of logs. Grass grows in the streets, chickens peck in the furrows.

You are lodged in a house. With the Brodelshchikovs. Simple folk with many children. They are aghast at your appearance, don't speak the same Russian as you. Don't answer any of your questions, the wife waves her arms around when she sees you coming in without wiping your shoes on the grass.

Mur who checks in a week later calls you an idiot, worthless. He insults you, shouts at you, orders you to go the next day to Chistopol, not to return without being assigned a lodging in that city.

You promise though you no longer have the strength to move, suggest you just have to be patient, wait: Chistopol will one day connect to Yelabuga.

You are going crazy, becoming mad without knowing it. Any pretext seems good not to move again. The constant search for lodging has exhausted you. Your legs are incapable of taking you farther than the first furrow.

The poverty in Yelabuga suits your ghastly appearance.

To leave Yelabuga or stay there in any case doesn't depend on you but on the decision of the NKVD which will discuss your case in ten days.

Ten days to endure Mur's bad mood, to scratch the furrows with your bare hands to dig up some potatoes forgotten by the farmers, ten days to wait for a sign from Pasternak to know if he can help you.

You live from day to day, do nothing to try to change the course of things. You desire nothing since they returned your package to Sergei with the note 'Not on the list'. Not on any list after consulting the rosters of all the prisons in Russia. Your husband has vanished. Vanished in the administrative fog.

'There are plenty of reasons to hang oneself,' you say again to Mur who becomes furious at your passivity.

You lean on that phrase so as not to reflect.

How to make him understand that leaving Yelabuga means turning your back on death, the only escape for you.

You fought to live, now you are fighting to no longer live. You were sure you would be saved by poetry and now here you are in hell because of poetry.

Learning of your plight, Pasternak intervenes with the NKVD which promises to look at your case.

Mur demands you attend the meeting that will take place in Chistopol the next day. You don't dare disobey him, and take the boat despite your terror of water.

Leaning against the wall for hours outside the room where the men and women you don't know discuss your fate, you look like a butterfly pinned in a shadowbox. The wall is too thick to capture the words exchanged inside.

Their verdict, you are sure of it, will be negative. Condemned to live in Yelabuga, to die there, to be buried there. An end appropriate to your destiny. The places where you've lived have always been imposed on you. Scarcely settled in a town and a house, you had to leave. So many moves in so few years, so many scattered objects and loves. The only constant, the dust, the same everywhere. As if you carried it in your suitcases, between the pages of your books, under your skin.

The same dust and the same man. Sergei, the only fixed element in your existence. Kept out of love and laziness because the others didn't keep you?

You were devastated, 15 years ago, when having learned of your affair with Rodzevich he wanted a divorce. You couldn't sleep, lost the will to live, begged forgiveness, gave up the lover but kept the child.

Rodzevich, an always open wound.

A final mute encounter in a hotel room.

He had spread your arms, crucified beneath him, moved in you without making a single sound, his eyes in yours as if to carry you away on his retinas. Brought you to ecstasy. His hand on your mouth stifled your cry.

Waiting for the end of the discussions behind the closed door is beyond your strength. Beyond your strength to confront Mur's anger and reproaches. You have only one desire: run away and put an end to your life.

What excuse can you offer to leave?

Would the policewoman who is watching you understand if you said to her: 'Excuse me, madame, may I go home so I can hang myself?'

You know you can expect nothing from this meeting.

Your country doesn't love you, its inhabitants don't love you.

Horizon obstructed. No work: the Writers Union hesitates to hire the wife of a man who fought with the Whites. The manager of the canteen rejected your offer to wash dishes, to wash the plates of your colleagues.

Speaking about you, the day after your suicide, a woman who had run into you that day in the hall of the NKVD says she had seen you hunched on the bench, humble, frightened, and that you had left before the end of the discussions and a decision that could have been in your favour.

Outside the sun is right above. Stuck under your feet, your shadow is neither in front nor behind you. A reassuring impression: no one is following you. You head for the boat landing, back to Yelabuga. You lower your arms, you are no longer capable of crossing swords with your times.

Having arrived on the opposite shore, you walk briskly then run at the sight of the grey roof, the grey walls of the Brodelshchikovs' house, run toward your death. Your past is erased as you approach your lodgers' house: Sergei, Alya, Mur, Rodzevich, Pasternak and all the others are only imaginary memories, necessary stopovers to reach your goal.

'The first one to leave suffers less in love,' according to a saying. You are going to apply it to the world and to the times that have mistreated you. You have decided to pre-empt death.

Grey gulls follow in the same direction. You are on familiar ground. An almost fraternal place. You know the number of furrows, know the exact hour when the night turns the hill and the cypress sharpened into a pencil blue.

A beam, a chair, and a rope await you between the walls of the garret. You just have to assemble them to end all your problems. To rest.

A well-deserved death, battling your times has exhausted you.

The loud bang of the chair falling over alerts the owners of the house. They come running, find you hanging from the ceiling, make the sign of the cross instead of taking you down. Touching a dead body brings bad luck.

Their shouts arouse the entire village. Everyone runs to the same house. No one left in the fields. Birds fly around in closed circles above the same roof.

Returning in the evening and seeing the crowd in front of the door, Mur knows what is waiting for him. You kept telling him you were going to hang yourself.

Prevented from going in, he leaves with his head lowered, seeks refuge at a friend's, won't attend your burial. No one but unknowns around the grave in a corner of the village cemetery, without a marker, without a cross, without a name, on 31 August 1941.

They don't know who you are, have never held one of your books in their hands, nor read a line of your poetry.

'An old woman like any other old woman', that's all that you are to them.

Gone with bare feet under that earth that you dug with your
bare hands to feed your son.

Dead leaves on your grave
It smells like winter
Hear me, oh dead
[. . .]
You laugh under your travelling pilgrim
The moon is high . . .

An appeal to friends to take care of Mur, among the three letters found on the table.

You beg them not to leave him alone and to take him to Chistopol. 'I want him to live and continue his studies. He was lost with me.'

'Bring him in, dear Aseev,' you write to the president of the Writers Union. 'Consider him your son. There are 50 rubles in my bag, and if you try to sell all my things . . . '

You ask him to love him, to take care of him: 'His health isn't good . . . '

'Forgive me, Murlyga,' you write lastly. 'I am no longer myself. I love you madly. Know that I could not continue living. Tell Papa and Alya if you see them that I loved them up to the last minute but that I am at a dead end.'

Aseev refused to take care of Mur, refused to keep Marina Tsvetaeva's archives.

Enrolled in the literature department in Moscow, Mur would later write novels in French and Russian; called up by the army, he was killed in 1944, three years after the death of his mother.

Alya spent eight years in deportation before being freed. Arrested again and sentenced to life in the Far North, she was pardoned in 1955 and allowed to live in Moscow.

Executed on 16 October 1941, Sergei Efron survived his wife by two months.

1892. 26 September: birth of Marina Ivanovna Tsvetaeva in Moscow. The daughter of the art historian Ivan Tsvetaev (founder of the Alexander III Museum of Fine Arts, known from 1937 as the Pushkin Museum), a widower, the father of two children, and of Maria Mein, a pianist.

1894. Birth of her sister Anastasia, called Assia.

1898-1899. Marina is enrolled in a music school. Her mother wanted her to become a musician. She learns French at the age of seven.

1902. The family goes to Italy, to Nervi, near Genoa, so Maria Mein can receive treatment for tuberculosis.

1903. Ivan Tsvetaev returns to Moscow. The girls, Assia and Marina, attend a French-language boarding school in Lausanne.

1904. The girls spend the summer in the Black Forest with their parents. In the autumn, Marina enrols in a school in Fribourg. She writes poems in German.

1906. 5 July: death of Maria Mein, Marina's mother. Marina attends several boarding schools in Moscow. Summers spent in Tarusa, near Kaluga, 150 kilometres from Moscow, in their vacation home. Marina develops a passion for Pushkin, Heine, Goethe and Hölderlin.

1909. At the age of 16, in the summer Marina goes alone to France to see Sarah Bernhardt in *l'Aiglon*, her favourite play. She worships Napoleon—and lives on rue Bonaparte. Studies Old French literature at the Sorbonne.

1910. Publication of her first collection, *Vecherny Albom* [Evening album], which elicits a rave review by Maximilian Voloshin, who would introduce her in literary circles and whom she would affectionately call 'My spiritual father'.

1911. In the spring, when she is invited to the home of Max Voloshin in Koktebel, in Crimea, she meets her future husband, Sergei Efron, whom she would marry on 27 January 1912, in Moscow, against the wishes of her family.

1912. February: publication of Marina's second collection, *Volshebnyi fonar* [The magic lantern]. 5 September: birth of her daughter Ariadna Efron, called Alya.

1913. 30 August: death of her father Ivan Tsvetaev.

1914. World War I: Sergei Efron leaves for the front as a nurse despite his bad health (tuberculosis). Affair with Sophia Parnok, lesbian poet, seven years her elder.

1915. Marina produces the collection *Youthful Verses*. July: in Koktebel, Marina meets Osip Mandelstam (born in 1891).

1916. Production of the cycles *Insomnia, Poems for Akhmatova, Poems for Blok, Verses about Moscow*.

1917. Sergei Efron fights with the White Army. Marina Tsvetaeva writes *The Demesne of the Swans*, around 100 poems celebrating the White Army. 13 April: birth of her second daughter, Irina.

1918. Very harsh living conditions in Moscow. Marina Tsvetaeva works for five and a half months at Narkomnats (People's Commissariat of Nationalities).

1919. Marina forms a bond with a group of young actors at the studios of the Moscow Art Theatre. She writes several plays in verse, deliberately 'aristocratic', the longest of which is dedicated to an episode in the life of Casanova: *Phoenix*. Passionate friendship with the young actress Sonia Holliday.

1920. 16 February: death of her daughter Irina (starvation).

1921. She writes the cycle *Separation* for her husband. In July, after three years, first news of Sergei Efron. 7 August: death of the poet Alexander Blok. Last poems to Blok.

1922. May: departure with her daughter for Berlin where she is to meet her husband. Stay in Berlin from 11 June to 31 July 1922. Beginning of a long correspondence with Boris Pasternak, who was enthusiastic when he read *Milestones*. Marina writes 'A Downpour of Light', an essay dedicated to Pasternak. 1 August: arrival of the Efron family in Czechoslovakia. Financial aid from the Czech government, within the framework of Russian Action. The family settles in Mokropsy, a village outside Prague. September: Tsvetaeva meets Anna Teskova who manages the Russian emigre aid fund and with whom she would correspond for 17 years until she returns to the USSR.

1923. Falls madly in love with Konstantin Rodzevich, the 'hero' of the 'Poem of the Mountain' and 'The Poem of the End'.

1924. Publication of the verse-narrative *Mólodets* [The swain], which she would translate herself into French. Composes the cycle *In the Inmost Hour of the Soul*.

1925. 1 February: birth of her son Georgy, whom she called Mur. 31 October: the family leaves for Paris, to the 19th arrondissement. She writes *The Ratcatcher*.

1926. Brief stay in London in March. Writes 'The Poet On the Critic', her first theoretical piece. Summer: vacation in Saint-Gilles-sur-Vie, in the Vendée. Composes two major poems: 'From the Sea', and 'An Attempt at a Room'. With the intervention of Pasternak, Rainer Maria Rilke sends Marina *Duino Elegies* and *Sonnets to Orpheus*. This is the beginning of the famous and intense three-way correspondence, *Letters: Summer 1926*. Autumn: the family moves to Bellevue. 29 December: death of Rilke.

1927. The Efron family settles in Meudon. Marina writes 'New Year's Greeting', a letter-poem addressed to Rilke. Composes 'Air Poem,' an attempt at a poetic reconstruction of Lindbergh's crossing of the Atlantic. September: Assia arrives from Moscow to visit her sister: she finds her in a state of deep physical and mental lethargy. Pasternak then attempts to intervene to enable Tsvetaeva to return to the USSR.

1928. Passionate friendship with a young Russian emigre poet, Nikolay Gronsky. Publication in Paris of the collection *After Russia*. 7 November: meets Mayakovsky in Paris. Tsvetaeva, who pays homage to his poetic force, antagonizes emigre circles.

1929. Short trip to Brussels. Essay on the painter Natalia Goncharova.

1930. 14 April: suicide of Mayakovsky. Marina dedicates a cycle of poems to him.

1931. Cycle of poems to Pushkin. Writes *History of a Dedication*, in which she recounts her memories of Mandelstam. End of Czech subsidies.

1932. Dire financial situation for the Efron family. Move to Clamart. Essays on art: *The Poet and Time*, in *Art in the Light of Conscience*. *Letter to the Amazon* (written in French), addressed to Natalie Clifford Barney. Writes 'A Living Word About a Living Man', in homage to Voloshin, who died on 11 August.

1933. Against her will, Marina turns to prose. Sergei Efron manages the Union for Repatriation, a Pro-Soviet organization that encourages emigres to return to the USSR.

1934. 8 January: death of Biely. Publication of 'Women of the Flagellant Sect'. October: the Efron family leaves Clamart for Vanves. 21 November: death of Nicolay Gronsky.

1935. Efron starts working for the Soviet secret service. June: a delegation of Russian writers arrives in Paris to attend an international meeting against fascism. Pasternak was present.

1936. May: invited to Belgium to present a reading of her poems, Tsvetaeva reads among others 'My Father and His Museum' and 'Memories of Kuzmin'.

Spanish War: Sergei clandestinely recruits for the International Brigades. Beginning of the great trials of Moscow, aiming to eliminate all opponents of Stalin.

1937. 15 March: Alya leaves for the USSR. Marina translates poems by Pushkin into French for the centenary of his death. Publication of *Moi Pushkin - My Pushkin*. Following the death of the actress Sonia Holliday, she writes *The Tale of Sonechka*.

Sergei Efron is involved in the assassination of a GPU agent who had deserted. He must leave clandestinely for Moscow on 10 October.

1938. Tsvetaeva remains alone in France with her son Mur. She begins making plans to join her husband and daughter. Summer: she abandons her apartment in Vanves for a room in the Hôtel Innova, 32, boulevard Pasteur. 29 September: Munich Accords. *Poems to Czechoslovakia.* Intense correspondence with Anna Teskova throughout the winter 1938-1939.

1939. 15 March: invasion of Czechoslovakia by German troops. 12 June: departure from Le Havre for Moscow with her son. The reunited family spends the summer in Bolshevo, where the NKVD lodged agents returning from abroad. 27 August: arrest of Alya at the age of 27. (Alya would spend 16 years in prison and in exile before being released in 1955. Until her death in 1975, she did everything she could to ensure that her mother's work would be recognized). 10 October: arrest of Sergei Efron.

1940. Does translations to survive, thanks to the help of Pasternak. Tsvetaeva spends the winter and spring in a Writers Union house.

1941. 6 and 7 June: meets with Anna Akhmatova. 22 June: German troops cross the border of the Soviet Union. 18 August: Tsvetaeva and her son are evacuated to Yelabuga, in Tatary. 31 August: Marina Tsvetaeva ends her life (by hanging) at the age of 49. 4 September: Mur volunteers to fight at the front. He is killed in July 1944 in Latvia. 16 October: Sergei Efron is executed.